"I am the boss, Miss Andrews," Hugo reminded her. From between his teeth. **"You are the employee. Everything about the way you are speaking to me is disrespectful, not to mention foolish. Why would you try to antagonize the person who pays your spectacularly generous salary?"**

Eleanor's frown smoothed out a bit, though she didn't precisely soften. And still, Hugo wanted to taste that faint crease between her brows, where the edge of her fringe kissed her skin the way he wanted to do.

"In point of fact, I won't be paid for two weeks," she said after a moment, as if she couldn't help herself. Maybe she really couldn't.

He couldn't have said why that notion washed through him like a new sort of heat.

"A notable distinction," Hugo murmured.

And then, because he loved nothing more than complicating any given situation beyond repair, the better to make it worse, he kis

And then they were tasted like magic.

D0019992

USA TODAY bestselling and RITA® Award–nominated author **Caitlin Crews** loves writing romance. She teaches her favorite romance novels in creative writing classes at places like UCLA Extension's prestigious Writers' Program, where she finally gets to utilize the MA and PhD in English literature she received from the University of York in England. She currently lives in California, with her very own hero and too many pets. Visit her at caitlincrews.com.

Books by Caitlin Crews

Harlequin Presents

Castelli's Virgin Widow
At the Count's Bidding

Scandalous Royal Brides

The Prince's Nine-Month Scandal
The Billionaire's Secret Princess

Wedlocked!

Bride by Royal Decree
Expecting a Royal Scandal

One Night With Consequences

The Guardian's Virgin Ward

The Billionaire's Legacy

The Return of the Di Sione Wife

Secret Heirs of Billionaires

Unwrapping the Castelli Secret

Scandalous Sheikh Brides

Protecting the Desert Heir
Traded to the Desert Sheikh

The Chatsfield

Greek's Last Redemption

Visit the Author Profile page at Harlequin.com for more titles.

Caitlin Crews

UNDONE BY THE BILLIONAIRE DUKE

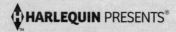

Recycling programs
for this product may
not exist in your area.

ISBN-13: 978-0-373-06105-1

Undone by the Billionaire Duke

First North American Publication 2017

Copyright © 2017 by Caitlin Crews

All rights reserved. Except for use in any review, the reproduction or utilization of this work in whole or in part in any form by any electronic, mechanical or other means, now known or hereinafter invented, including xerography, photocopying and recording, or in any information storage or retrieval system, is forbidden without the written permission of the publisher, Harlequin Enterprises Limited, 225 Duncan Mill Road, Don Mills, Ontario M3B 3K9, Canada.

This is a work of fiction. Names, characters, places and incidents are either the product of the author's imagination or are used fictitiously, and any resemblance to actual persons, living or dead, business establishments, events or locales is entirely coincidental.

This edition published by arrangement with Harlequin Books S.A.

For questions and comments about the quality of this book, please contact us at CustomerService@Harlequin.com.

® and TM are trademarks of Harlequin Enterprises Limited or its corporate affiliates. Trademarks indicated with ® are registered in the United States Patent and Trademark Office, the Canadian Intellectual Property Office and in other countries.

Printed in U.S.A.

UNDONE BY THE BILLIONAIRE DUKE

To Maisey Yates and Nicole Helm for encouraging my flights of fancy—like rearing horses and billowing cloaks, oh my!

CHAPTER ONE

ELEANOR ANDREWS WAS certain that she could handle the likes of Hugo Grovesmoor, and no matter that no one had ever quite managed to do so before in living memory. As the papers shrieked daily, the Twelfth Duke of Grovesmoor was not only known to be a terrible villain in every salacious way imaginable, he was *impossible*. Too wealthy. Too full of himself. And worse still, so appallingly and egregiously handsome that he'd essentially been born spoilt through, and had only descended further from there.

Into pure, hedonistic, and ruinous devilry. Usually with pictures.

And Eleanor was delivering herself directly into his clutches.

"Don't be so dramatic," her younger sister Vivi said with a sigh, sending her long and lively brunette curls slithering this way and that every time she exhaled. When all Eleanor had done was express the tiniest hint of concern about her brand-new role as governess to the poor seven-year-old in notorious Hugo's care.

As occasionally trying as Vivi was—and if Eleanor was honest with herself, it was more *often* than *occasionally*—Eleanor couldn't help but love her. Desperately. Vivi was all she had left after their parents had been killed years ago in the tragic car accident that had nearly claimed young Vivi's life, as well. Eleanor never forgot how close she'd come to losing Vivi, too.

"I don't think I was being dramatic at all," Eleanor replied. She chose not to point out that the opera heroine histrionics were usually Vivi's department. Surely that went without saying.

Vivi was addressing Eleanor through the mirror in the bedroom of the tiny, crowded, so-called "one-bedroom" flat they shared in one of London's less fashionable neighborhoods. The "one bedroom" in question being the space on the far side of a bookcase in the long room with a cramped kitchenette slung beneath the eaves on the other end. Vivi was applying a third, slick layer of mascara to her lashes, the better to emphasize the eyes one of her many boyfriends had once called *as warm and bright as new gold.* Eleanor had heard him—as had half the street in the village where they'd grown up as their distant cousin's charity cases after their parents had been killed and Vivi had finally gotten out of the hospital—given that the poor sod had been shouting it toward Vivi's window long after the pubs had closed, as pissed as he was poetic.

Vivi lowered the mascara wand and rolled said *new gold eyes.* "You won't actually *see* Hugo. You're going to be the governess of his ward who, let's face it, he can't possibly like that much. Given all that messy history. Why would he give either one of you the time of day?"

A dismissive wave of her hand encompassed all the salacious details everyone knew about Hugo Grovesmoor, thanks to the fascination the tabloids had always had with him.

Eleanor knew the three main points as well as anyone. The dramatic on-and-off relationship with beloved society darling Isobel Vanderhaven, whom everyone had been certain Hugo would ruin with his shocking brand of committed wickedness that even Isobel's innate goodness couldn't cure. The way Isobel had left him for good when pregnant with his best friend's Torquil's child, because, everyone agreed, love had finally triumphed over wickedness and Isobel deserved better. And Isobel's celebrated marriage to and subsequent tragic boating accident with said former best friend, which had resulted in famously reluctant Hugo being named the legal guardian of the child whose very existence had wrecked his chances with the lovely Isobel forever.

All this while the nation jeered, applauded, and mourned in turn, as if they knew all of these people and their pain personally.

"A man as rich as Hugo is dripping in properties and can't be expected to visit even half of them in the course of a year. Or even five years," Vivi said with the same nonchalance, and Eleanor reminded herself that her sister would know.

After all, Vivi was the one who'd spent time with Hugo Grovesmoor's sort of people. She was the one who'd attended the posh schools and while she hadn't exactly distinguished herself academically, she'd certainly had a sparkling social calendar that had carried over to her life in London. It was all in service to the glittering marriage they were both certain Vivi would manage to score any day now.

Vivi was eighteen months younger than Eleanor and the beauty of the pair of them. She had the sort of slim-hipped, smoky-eyed, lush-mouthed prettiness that left men struck dumb when they beheld her. Literally. Her wild curls gave the impression she'd just rolled out of someone's bed. Her just-wicked-enough smile hinted that she was up for any and all adventures and suggested that if a man played his cards right, that bed could be his.

And to think that after the accident, the doctors had doubted she'd ever walk again!

Vivi had proven herself to be more or less catnip for a certain sort of man. Usually one endowed with a great many estates and a bank account to match, even if, so far, she hadn't quite managed to break out of the "potential mistress" box.

Eleanor, on the other hand, went to very few parties while working at least one job and sometimes more, when things got rough. Because while Vivi was the pretty one, Eleanor had always been the sensible one. And while she'd had her moments of wishing she, too, could have been as effortlessly charming and undeniably pretty as her sister, Eleanor was twenty-seven now and had come to a place of peace with her role in life. They'd lost their parents and Eleanor couldn't bring them back. She couldn't change the many years of hospitals and surgeries that Vivi had survived. But she could take on a bit of a parental role with Vivi. She could hold down decent jobs and pay their bills.

Well. Vivi's bills. There was no point gussying up Eleanor in the sort of slinky, breathtakingly expensive clothes Vivi had to have to blend in with her highbrow friends—and *that sort of thing* required money. Money Eleanor had always made, one way or another.

This latest job—as governess to the most hated man in England—would be the most lucrative yet. It was why Eleanor had resigned from her current position as a front desk receptionist at a bustling architecture firm. Vivi had been the one to hear of the governess position through her high-flying set of friends, since men like the Duke did not exactly pin up adverts in the local pub. More important, she'd heard what the Duke intended to pay his governess. It was so much more than all the other jobs Eleanor had taken—combined—that she hardly dared do the math, lest it make her dizzy.

"The rumor is the Duke has dismissed all the governesses he's been sent. Being a distraction is apparently the top reason for getting sacked and, well..."

Vivi had shrugged with a regret that had not struck Eleanor as being entirely sincere. Her small, perfect, perky breasts had moved enticingly behind the filmy little silk dress she'd worn to some or other desperately fashionable soirée that evening, as if in an approving chorus.

"But you *might just be perfect!"*

The sleek agency that had handled the interview had agreed, and here Eleanor was, packing up her case for the trip into the wilds of the Yorkshire moors to what had to be the most overwrought of all the ducal properties in England. Groves House, as the sprawling dark mansion was quaintly called as if it wasn't large enough to merit its own postal code, had been looming over its vast swathe of the brooding moors for centuries.

"A governess is a lowly member of his household staff, Eleanor," Vivi was saying now, with another eye roll. "Not a guest. It's highly unlikely you'll encounter Hugo Grovesmoor at all."

That was more than fine with Eleanor. She was immune to star power and the sense of self-importance that went along with it. She told herself so all the way up on the train the next morning as it hurtled at high speeds toward deepest Yorkshire.

She hadn't gone to the north of England since she was a child and their parents had still been alive. Eleanor had vague memories of traipsing about the walls that surrounded the ancient city of York in a chilly summer fog, with no idea, then, how quickly everything would change.

But there was no point heading down that sort of sentimental road now, she told herself sternly as she waited in the brisk October cold at the York rail station for one of the slower, more infrequent local trains out into the far reaches of the countryside. Life went on. That was just what it did, wholly heedless and uncaring.

No matter what anyone might have lost along the way.

When Eleanor arrived at the tiny little train station in remote Grovesmoor Village, she expected to be met as planned. But the train platform in the middle of nowhere was empty. There was nothing but Eleanor, the blustering October wind, and the remains of the morning's fog. Not exactly an encouraging beginning.

Eleanor cast a bit of a grim eye at the case she'd packed with what she'd thought she'd need for the first six weeks she'd agreed to spend at Groves House without any break. It was only the one case. Vivi needed to travel with bags upon bags, but then again, she had a *wardrobe*. Eleanor had no such problems. And no excuses. It took a second or two to pull up a map on her mobile and find it was a twenty-to-thirty-minute walk to the only stately manor in the area. Groves House.

"Best set off, then," she muttered to herself.

She heaved her heavy shoulder bag higher up on her shoulder, grabbed the handle of her roller bag and tugged on it, and strode off with every confidence in the world. Or every appearance of confidence, anyway, she amended when she walked for five minutes down the road only to realize she should have headed in the opposite direction, away from the quaint little town arranged on either side of a slow river.

Once headed in the right direction, Eleanor tried to channel Maria Von Trapp as she trudged along the lonely country road that wound further and further into the fog and the gloom. She marched on, aware of her breathing in the otherwise still afternoon and very little else. She'd lived so long in the hectic rush of London now that she'd almost forgotten the particular quiet of country lane, particularly one that seemed to be swallowed up by moors in all directions and peaks here and there that she expected would have names. If only she'd researched them.

She found the turnoff for Groves House between two stone pillars and started up the drive. It wound about just as much as the road had, and was only differentiated from the lane she'd left behind by its absence of hedges and proper stone walls. And its slight incline straddled by lines of stout and watchful trees. She'd lost track of how many turns she'd taken and how far she'd gone from the road when she looked out in front of her and saw the house at last.

Nothing could have prepared her.

The house loomed there on the far ridge. It was rambling, yes, a jumble of stone and self-importance, but none of the pictures she'd seen had done it justice. There was something about it that made a raw sort of lump catch there in her throat. There was something about the way its interior lights scraped at the gloomy afternoon that seemed to speak to her, though she couldn't think why.

She found she couldn't look away.

It was not a welcoming house. It was not a *house* at all, for that matter. It was much too large and starkly forbidding. And yet somehow, as it gleamed there against the fall night as if daring the dark to do its worst, the only word that echoed inside Eleanor's head was *perfect*.

Something rang in her then, low and long, like a bell.

She didn't know why she couldn't seem to catch her breath when she started walking again, her case seeming heavier in her grip as she headed further up the hill.

And that was when she heard the thunder of hoof beats, bearing down on her.

Like fate.

His Grace the Duke of Grovesmoor, known to what few friends he had left and the overly familiar press as Hugo, found fewer and fewer things cleared his head these days. Drink made his skull hurt. Extreme sports had lost their thrill now that his death would mean the end of the Grovesmoor line of succession after untold centuries, tossing the whole dukedom into the hands of grasping, far-removed cousins who'd been salivating over the ducal properties and attendant income for perhaps the entire sweep of its history.

Even indiscriminate sex, once his favorite go-to for obliteration on a grand scale, had lost its charm now that his every so-called "indiscretion" went rabbiting off to the papers before the sheets had gone cold to tell further tales in the nation's favorite narrative. Evil, soulless Hugo, despoiler of saints and heroes, etc. He was either glutting himself in excess to hide from his dark regrets or he was so extraordinarily shallow that a shag or two was all he was capable of. The stories were all the same and always so damned boring.

It galled him to admit it, but the tabloids might actually have won.

The particular horse he rode today—the pride of his stables, he'd been informed, as if he gave a toss—liked him as little as he liked it, which meant he found himself rampaging across the moors very much as if he'd sprung forth from a bloody eighteenth century novel.

All he needed was a billowing cloak.

But no matter how far he rode, there was no escaping himself. Or his head and all his attendant regrets.

The vicious creature he rode clearly knew it. They'd been playing a little domination game for weeks now, raging across the whole of Hugo's Yorkshire estate.

So when Hugo saw the figure slinking along in the shadows up the drive to Groves House, all he could think was that it was something *different* in the middle of an otherwise indistinguishably gray afternoon.

God knew Hugo was desperate for anything different.

A different past. A different reputation—because

who could have foreseen what his shrugging off all those early tabloid stories would lead to?

He wanted a different *him*, really, but that had never been on offer.

Hugo was the Twelfth Duke of Grovesmoor whether he liked it or did not, and the title was the important thing about him. The only important thing, his father had been at pains to impress upon him all his life. Unless he bankrupted his estates and rid himself of the title altogether, or died while engaged in some or other irresponsible pursuit, Hugo would simply be another notation in the endless long line of dukes bearing the same title and a healthy dollop of the same blood. His father had always claimed that knowledge had brought him solace. Peace.

Hugo was unfamiliar with either.

"If you're a poacher, you're doing a remarkably sad job of it," he said when he drew close to the stranger on his property. "You really should at least *try* to sneak about, surely. Instead of marching up the front drive without the slightest attempt at subterfuge."

He reined in the stroppy horse and enjoyed the dramatic way he then reared a bit right in front of the person creeping up his drive.

It was then that he realized his intruder was a woman.

And not just any woman.

Hugo was renowned for his women. Bloody Isobel, of course, like a stain across his life—but all the other ones, too. Before Isobel and after. But they all had the same things in common: they were considered beautiful by all and sundry and wanted, usually quite badly, to be photographed next to him. That meant fake breasts, whitened teeth, extensions to thicken their silky hair, varnished nails and careful lipstick and fake lashes and all the rest of it. So years had passed since he'd seen a real woman at all, unless she worked for him. His crotchety old housekeeper, for example, who he kept on because Mrs. Redding was always as deeply disappointed when he appeared in the tabloids as his father had been. It felt so comfortable, Hugo often thought. Like a lovely, well-worn hair shirt tucked up next to his skin.

The woman who stared up at him now, looking nowhere near as shocked or outright terrified as Hugo imagined he would be if he'd found himself on the underside of a rearing horse, was not in the least bit beautiful.

Or if she was, she'd gone to significant lengths to disguise it. Her hair was scraped back into a tight brown bun that made his own head ache just looking at it, without a single flyaway to suggest she was actually human. Even her fringe was ruthlessly cut across her forehead to military precision. She wore a bulky, puffy sort of jacket that covered her from chin to calf and made her look roughly the size of one of the grand, gnarled old oaks dotting the property. She clutched a large black bag over her shoulder and tugged a rolling case along behind her, and she had death grips on both. Her cheeks looked flushed with the cold and there was no denying she had a delicate nose a great many of his own ancestors would have envied, given the curse of what was known as The Grovesmoor Beak that seemed to afflict the females in the line unfairly.

But most of what struck him was the expression on her face.

Because it looked a great deal like a scowl.

Which was, of course, impossible, because he was Hugo Grovesmoor and the women who usually crept onto his various properties without invitation found the very idea of him—or to be more precise, of his net worth—so marvelously attractive that they never stopped smiling. Ever.

This woman looked as if she'd crack in half if she attempted the smallest grin.

"I'm not poaching, I'm a governess." Her voice was cool, and something else that Hugo couldn't identify. "My ride from the train station didn't materialize or I assure you, I wouldn't be marching anywhere, much less up this very long drive. Uphill."

It dawned on him then. That "something else" in her voice he hadn't been able to place. It was *annoyance*.

Hugo found it delightful. No one was *annoyed* with him. They might hate him and call him Satan and other such tedious things, but they were never *annoyed*.

"I should have introduced myself, I think," he said merrily, as the bastard horse danced murderously beneath him. The woman did not appear to know her own danger, so close to sharp hooves and the thoroughbred's temper tantrums. Or, more likely, she didn't care, as she was too busy trying to win a staring contest with Hugo. "Since you're lurking about the property."

"It is not lurking to walk up the front drive," she replied crisply. "By definition."

"I am Hugo Grovesmoor," he told her. "No need to curtsey. After all, I'm, widely held to be a great and terrible villain."

"I had no intention of curtseying."

"I prefer to think of myself as an antihero, of course. Surely that merits a bow. Or perhaps a small nod?"

"My name is Eleanor Andrews and I'm the latest in what I've been told is a long line of governesses," the woman told him from the depths of that quilted monstrosity she wore. "I intend to be the last, and if I'm not very much mistaken, the way to ensure that happens is to keep my distance."

Hugo was used to women making similar announcements. *You're terrible,* they'd coo, lashes batting furiously. *I'm keeping my distance from you.* This usually led directly to the sort of indiscriminate evenings from which he was now abstaining.

He had the lowering realization that this woman—wrapped up in a hideous puffy coat with her chin jutting forth and a scowl across her face—might actually mean it.

"Your Grace," he murmured.

"I beg your pardon?"

"You should address me as Your Grace, particularly when you imagine you are taking me to task. It adds that extra little touch of pointed disrespect which I find I cannot live without."

If Eleanor Andrews was appropriately mortified by the fact she'd addressed a peer of the realm—who happened to also be her new boss—so inappropriately, she gave no sign. If anything she seemed to pull herself up straighter in her vast, quilted shroud, and made no attempt to wipe off that scowl.

"A thousand apologies, Your Grace," she said crisply, as if she wasn't in the least bit intimidated by him. It made something in Hugo…shift. "I was expecting a ride from the train station. Not a walk in the chilly countryside."

"Exercise improves the mind as well as the body, I'm told," he replied, merrily enough. "I myself was blessed with a high metabolism and a keen intelligence, so I've never had to put such things to the test. But we can't all be so lucky."

There was enough light that he could tell that there was a remarkable sort of honey in the brown of this woman's eyes as they glittered furiously at him. He couldn't imagine why that shocked him, but it did. That there should be anything soft about such a bristling, black-clad, evidently humorless female.

That he should notice it.

"Are you suggesting that I am not as lucky as you?" she asked, with exactly the sort of repressed fury Hugo would expect to hear from a woman he'd just obliquely called fat.

"That depends on whether or not you imagine that

the storied life of a pampered duke is a matter of luck and circumstance. Rather than fate."

"Which do you think it is?"

Hugo nearly smiled at that. He couldn't have said why. It was something to do with the way her eyes gleamed and her surprisingly intriguing mouth was set, flashing more of that annoyance straight at him.

"I appreciate you thinking of my well-being," she said with what he was forced to concede was admirable calm, all that flashing annoyance notwithstanding. "Your Grace."

Hugo grinned down at her, hoping she found having to look so far up at him as irritating as he would have.

"I wasn't aware that the last governess left, though I can't say I'm surprised. She was a fragile little thing. All anime eyes and protracted spells of weeping in the east wing, or so I'm told. I'm allergic to female tears, you understand. I've developed a sixth sense. When a woman cries in my vicinity, I am instantly and automatically transported to the other side of the planet."

Eleanor only gazed back at him. "I'm not much of a crier."

Hugo waited.

"Your Grace," he prodded her again when it was clear she had no intention of saying it. "I wouldn't insist upon such formality but it does seem to chafe, doesn't it? How republican of you. And really, Eleanor, you can't expect to mold a young mind to your will and provide fodder for the therapy bills I'll be expected to pay out from her trust if you can't remember the courtesy of a simple form of address. It's as if you've never met a duke before."

She blinked. "I haven't."

"I'm not a particularly good representative. I'm far too scandalous, as mentioned. Perhaps you've heard." He laughed when she did a terrible job of keeping her face blank. "I see you have. No doubt you're an avid fan of the tabloids and their daily regurgitations of my many sins. I can only hope to be even half as colorful in person."

"And it's Miss Andrews."

It was Hugo's turn to blink. "Sorry?"

"I would prefer it if you call me Miss Andrews." She nodded then, a faint inclination of her head, which he supposed was as close to any kind of recognition as he'd get. *Your Grace.*

Something moved in him then, far worse than a mere shift. It felt raw. Dangerous.

Impossible.

"Let me clear something up from the start, Miss Andrews," he said, while his terrible horse tried to trick him into easing his hold on the reins. "I'm exactly as bad as they say. Worse. I ruin lives with a mere crook of my finger. Yours. The child's. Random pedestrians minding their own business in the village square. I have so many victims it's a bit of luck, really, that the country still stands. I'm my own blitzkrieg. If you have a problem with that, Mrs. Redding will be happy to replace you. You need only say the word."

If that affected this maddening woman in any way, she hid it behind her mountainous coat and that equally dour gray scarf.

"I told you, I have no intention of being replaced." He couldn't say he liked the exaggerated note of patience in her voice then. "Certainly not of my own volition. Whether you wish to replace me or not is, of course, entirely up to you."

"I might." He arched a brow. "I do detest poachers."

She eyed him as if he was her charge, not his ward. *His ward.* He hated even thinking those words. He hated even more the fact that Isobel had done exactly what she'd spitefully promised she'd do, time and again: kept her hooks in him even from beyond the grave.

"You should do as you please, Your Grace, and something tells me you will—"

"It is my gift. My expression of my best self."

"—but I might suggest you see how I handle the child before you send me packing."

The child. His ward.

Hugo hated that he was required to think about anyone's welfare at all when he cared so little for his own. He had extensive staff in place, paid handsomely to think about the health and happiness of all his many tenants and other staff members and various employees, leaving him free to lounge about being as useless as he liked.

Which—he'd read in the papers and heard from

a chorus of people who would know, like his own dearly departed father—was all he was good for.

The girl, however, was a different sort of responsibility than real estate in Central London or a selection of islands in the Pacific or a coffee plantation in Africa or whatever else was in his holdings.

To say Hugo bitterly resented this was putting it mildly.

"What an excellent idea," he murmured. "I'll see she's waiting for you in the great hall when you finally make it to the house. It shouldn't be long. Five minutes' walk if you keep a good pace."

"You must be joking."

"Fair enough. Ten minutes' walk if your legs are shorter than mine, I suppose. I'm afraid I can't tell, as you appear to be wearing enough goosedown to leave the entire goose population of the United Kingdom shivering and bare. Assuming that's what's making you so…" He nodded at her voluminous black tent. "Puffy."

"Your hospitality is truly inspiring, Your Grace," she said after a moment, and the fact she managed to keep her face and voice smooth…poked at him.

He didn't like it.

Just as he really, *really* didn't like the fact that he couldn't remember the last time anyone or anything had managed to get beneath his skin.

"That is, as ever, my only goal," he replied.

And then, because he could—because he'd dedicated himself to being every bit as awful as he was expected to be, if not worse—Hugo spun the horse around, galloped off, and left the problematic Miss Eleanor Andrews there to find her own damned way to his house.

And his ward.

And this life of his that he'd never wanted, but had inherited anyway. Some would claim he'd earned it. That he deserved it and more.

That it really was fate, not luck, after all.

Hugo knew it didn't matter. He was trapped in it all the same.

CHAPTER TWO

FIFTEEN MINUTES LATER, Eleanor trudged up to the front of the house at last.

The front door itself rose forbiddingly up over a circular area directly in front of it that was paved with smooth stones and accented by the remnants of a garden turning brown as winter approached.

It seemed like an omen. Though Eleanor did not permit herself to believe in such things, of course.

The closer she'd got to the house, the more she'd wondered exactly why she'd agreed to any of this in the first place. Was it truly necessary that she isolate herself in this creepy old manor house? Was all that lovely money really worth marooning herself in Yorkshire with a man she'd never imagined she'd meet face to face—and didn't want to meet again, thank you?

And why couldn't Vivi do something for herself for a change?

But such thoughts made her feel disloyal. A little bit sick to her stomach. It felt like an act of betrayal when Vivi had come so close to losing her own life in that terrible accident. And had fought so hard to stay here. And walk again. Eleanor had been the only one left unscathed.

Sometimes she felt the guilt of that as if it was her own scar, slashed bright and hot across her whole body.

"Stop feeling sorry for yourself," she told herself briskly, pulling herself together as best she could. "You already took the position."

She rang the great and imposing bell that hung beside the door before she could think better of it, tugging on the slick old pull once. Then again.

It sounded long and low and deep, like some throwback to medieval times. She half expected knights in shining armor to come cantering up, wittering on about old King Arthur and ladies in lakes.

She was coming over all fanciful. That was what that man had done to her with his smirk and his amusement and his *mouth* when he was nothing but the same unsavory character she'd read about in the papers all these years. Only worse.

The fact that he was infinitely better-looking than any picture she'd ever seen of him didn't help. Worse, he was not nearly as fatuous as she'd imagined and he'd been entirely too sardonic besides. Her knees hadn't felt right since.

But as the door swung inward, she found herself staring not at a disgraceful duke in all his questionable glory, but down into the bright blue eyes and suspicious face of a little girl.

A little girl with silky red-gold hair plaited on either side of her head and a brace of adorable freckles across her nose. A little girl who made Eleanor's breath catch, because it was impossible to look at her and not see her very famous, very dead mother. Isobel Vanderhaven of the sunny smile and titian hair, who'd looked like everybody's best friend and the girl next door—if, that was, you happened to live next to one of her parents' rolling vineyards in South Africa.

"I don't need a governess," the child announced at once. In a tone that could only be called challenging.

"Of course you don't," Eleanor agreed, and the girl blinked. "Who *needs* a governess? But you are lucky enough to have one anyway."

The little girl considered her for a moment, as the October wind blustered and moaned, rushing in from the moors smelling of rain and winter.

"I'm Geraldine." Her lower lip protruded just slightly, and made her look her age, suddenly. "But you probably know that. They always know that."

"Of course I know your name," Eleanor said briskly. "I couldn't very well take a job if I didn't know the name of my charge, could I?"

It was clear to Eleanor that this child would keep her standing on the doorstep until the end of time if she didn't do something about it herself. So she pushed open the door with her free hand, and brushed straight past Geraldine, who watched her with a mixture of surprise and interest.

"They usually just stand in the drive, texting and whingeing," she piped up.

"Who is 'they'?" Eleanor reached past Geraldine once she'd stepped inside and shut the door, firmly, which took some doing because it outweighed her by approximately seven tons. And when she turned around to face the hall that had been waiting there behind her, she was glad the little girl didn't appear to be paying strict attention to her.

Because she was standing in a bloody castle.

Or close enough, anyway. Groves House had looked so grim and brooding from the outside, but here in the spacious foyer, it gleamed. Eleanor couldn't tell how it was doing that, precisely. Was there gold in the walls themselves? Was it the way the chandeliers hit all the paintings and the elegant furnishings and the rest of the things that seemed to clutter up rich people's foyers, that she'd only ever seen before on episodes of *Downton Abbey*?

"Everyone knows my name," Geraldine was saying with all the self-possession of the very young. "Sometimes they yell it at me in the village. You're the fifteenth governess so far, did you know that?"

"I did not."

"Mrs. Redding says I'm disobedient."

"What do you think?" Eleanor asked. "Are you?"

Geraldine looked a bit thrown by the question. "Maybe."

"Then you can stop, if you like." Eleanor eyed the mutinous little face before her and didn't see any disobedience. She saw a lonely little girl who'd lost her parents and had been sent off to live with a stranger. Eleanor could certainly relate. She ducked her chin so her face was closer to Geraldine's and whispered the thing that no one had ever bothered to say to her when she'd been heartsick and orphaned, waiting to find out if Vivi would make it through her latest surgery. "It won't matter either way, you know. Whether you're good or bad. I can already tell we'll be great friends and that means we always will. Friends don't change their minds about each other when things get tough, after all."

All Geraldine did was blink. Once, then again. But that was enough. Eleanor started unzipping her big coat.

"She's not any more disobedient than any other small human creature," came a male voice Eleanor wished she didn't recognize, wafting down the length of the hall as if it, too, was made of gold. And was set to shine. "She's seven. Let's not put the child in a cage so quickly, shall we?"

It took her a moment to find Hugo in all the dizzy brilliance of the bright foyer. But then there he was, sauntering out of one of the connected rooms toward the front door as if he hadn't a care in the world.

Because of course, he didn't.

He looked nothing like a duke should, Eleanor thought darkly. No Hooray Henry red trousers or Barbour slung just so for the most hated man in all of England. Not for Hugo. He came towards her in an old, battered pair of jeans. He had his hands thrust into the pockets like some kind of slumming American celebrity. He wore a T-shirt, cleverly ripped here and there, like those Eleanor had seen in the posh shops that Vivi preferred. It was the sort of T-shirt that would've looked like a soiled tissue on a lesser man. But Hugo hadn't been lying about his metabolism. Or anyway, that was how Eleanor tried to view the magnificent specimen of male beauty walking toward her then: in terms of his metabolism.

Because everything on Hugo Grovesmoor's body was cut to perfection as if he was another piece of statuary in his own hall. His chest was ridiculous, broad at the top and narrow near his hips and stunningly ridged in between. He looked as if he should be racing about in a loincloth, banging on about Sparta. Instead, his dark eyes were the precise shade of a lazy glass of whiskey, his dark hair looked very much as if he'd been galloping around in a bedchamber instead of on horseback, and that little curl in the corner of his mouth was nothing short of disastrous.

Because Eleanor could feel it everywhere. Lighting her up in places she'd long since forgotten about.

She didn't know what that dark, edgy thing was that wound around inside of her then. What she did know was that it was Hugo's fault.

"The child is already in a cage," Eleanor retorted before she could think better of it. She flicked a glance around the vast hall, which was even bigger and more magnificent at a second glance, and just as dizzying, from the plump chandeliers to the acrobatic sconces on the walls. "A large one, I grant you."

Hugo kept moving toward her, eventually coming to a stop a few feet away. And then they were all three standing there in various degrees of awkward-ness, right in front of the big front door.

It was worse when he was close, Eleanor was forced to admit. It made her feel raw and unsteady inside. It had been bad enough when he was up on the back of that giant horse, hooves flailing every which way and that mocking voice of his like a weapon, but Hugo even closer was confusing. Eleanor eyed him balefully, as if that might do something about that bright nonsense sloshing around inside of her and making her feel…things.

Way too many *things*.

In entirely too many places.

She told herself that it was only that she still had her big, heavy coat on. The coat was the reason she was flushed. Too warm. Almost itchy, somehow. It had nothing at all to do with him.

Next to her, Hugo did nothing to change the im-pression she'd had of him from across the hall. Or up on that horse, for that matter. And once the shock of his astonishing male beauty wore off—or, if she was more precise, dimmed a slight bit when she managed to breathe—she found that what really exuded from him like his own, very rich and unmistakable scent was all that arrogance.

That smile of his only deepened then. It was as if he could read her mind.

But he directed his attention to Geraldine. "Well?"

The little girl only shrugged, a sullen look on her cute little face.

"No point letting this one settle in like the oth-

ers, if you're only going to complain about it later."
Hugo's voice was…different, Eleanor thought. Not
exactly softer, but more careful.

She was so busy trying to figure out what the difference was that she almost missed what he'd said.

"I beg your pardon. Are we discussing my em-
ployment?"

Hugo slid that gaze of his back to her. Too lazy.
Too hot. She could feel it in too many places. More
than before, and hotter.

"*We* are." He raised a dark brow. "It appears you're
doing nothing but eavesdropping."

Eleanor's teeth hurt, and she unclenched them.
"It would be eavesdropping if I was hid behind one
of the flower arrangements, blending into all this
feverish decor." She forced herself to smile, and the
fact that it was difficult made her uneasy. More than
uneasy, but she did it anyway. "*I* am not eavesdropping. But *you* are being remarkably inappropriate."

"It's a bit of bad form to hurl accusations like that
at an innocent child, don't you think?" Hugo asked
lazily, and Eleanor had the strangest thought that he
was teasing her.

But why would the Duke of Grovesmoor tease
anyone, much less someone as insignificant as Eleanor, a governess he apparently no longer wished to
hire? She thrust that aside and concentrated on the
only part of this bizarre interaction that she could
control. Or try to control, anyway.

"I think all three of us are perfectly aware who
I'm speaking to." Eleanor gazed down at Geraldine

then, and this time her smile was genuine. "It won't hurt my feelings if you'd like me to leave, Geraldine. And I don't mind it if you say so to my face. But the Duke is very deliberately putting you in a position where you can act out his bad impulses, and that isn't fair."

"Life isn't fair," Hugo murmured, a bit too dark and smooth for Eleanor's peace of mind.

Eleanor ignored that, wishing it was as easy to ignore him. "It's also perfectly okay not to know," she told the little girl. "We met all of five minutes ago. If you'd like to take a little bit longer to make up your mind, that's fine."

"You say that with such authority," Hugo said. "Almost as if we stand in your house instead of mine."

Then he looked around as if he'd never laid eyes on the hall before in his life, when Eleanor knew full well that he'd been born here. Apparently, the Duke liked a bit of theater. She filed that away.

"But no," he continued, as if anyone had argued with him. "It's the same hall I remember from the whole of my benighted childhood, when governesses far stricter than you failed entirely to make me into a decent man. Portraits of my dreary ancestors lining the walls. Pedigrees as far as the eye can see. Grovesmoors in every direction and back again. Which would suggest that the authority lies with me and not you, would it not?"

"Funny," Eleanor said coolly, keeping her gaze fixed to his as if she wasn't the least bit intimidated.

Because she certainly shouldn't have been, and why should it matter to her that his gaze felt as intoxicating as it looked? "The agency is under the impression that in this situation, Geraldine has the authority."

"Do you think so?" Hugo asked with a dangerous sort of laziness in his voice, then.

She didn't know what he might have said then. Something like temper stormed about in that gaze of his, making her breath feel heavy and tight in her chest.

But she knew, somehow, that it wasn't temper. Not quite.

"I like her," Geraldine chimed in then. "I want her to stay."

The Duke didn't shift his eyes from Eleanor's.

"Your wish is my command, my favorite ward," he said in that same careful tone, and maybe Eleanor was the only one who could hear all those undercurrents. Or feel them, anyway. Swishing around inside of her as if she'd had entirely too much to drink.

As if he was a new brand of spirit served in far more than the usual measures.

Everything felt hot. Entirely too sharp, as if there were some unseen hand clenched around them, gripping them tight. This close, Eleanor was sure that she could feel the heat of the Duke's body, making that T-shirt of his seem sensible. Making her feel that much warmer and uncomfortable in her own skin.

It's only the coat, she told herself desperately, but he was still so close. And much too tall. He towered over her the same way he had on that damned horse, and she assured herself there was no particular reason she should have the image of its flailing hooves, rearing up over her, when it was only a man standing in front of her in an entryway. Just a man. No dangerous animal in sight.

She was sure he almost said something, but he didn't. Instead, he shifted. He pulled one hand out of his jeans pocket, and lifted it. That was all. If she'd seen a stranger do it on the street, she wouldn't have thought of it as any kind of gesture. It seemed accidental.

But it wasn't, she realized the next moment, because suddenly the hall was filled with people.

Geraldine was swept away in the care of two clucking nannies. Someone took Eleanor's bags, another person took her coat, and then suddenly there was a very neatly dressed, efficient-looking older woman bearing down on her with a tight smile on her mouth and her steel gray hair tucked back in a bun that looked a great deal like Eleanor's own.

"Mrs. Redding, I presume," Eleanor said as the woman drew close.

"Miss Andrews." The woman greeted her in the same briskly matter-of-fact tone Eleanor recognized from the telephone calls they'd had. "If you'll come with me."

As Eleanor followed her deeper into the depths of the great house, she realized that the Duke was nowhere to be seen. Then he'd disappeared in all the commotion.

She told herself she was relieved.

"I do apologize that there was no one waiting to collect you from the station," the housekeeper said as she strode through the maze of halls, not pausing for an instant to give Eleanor a glimpse of the splendor closing in on all sides. Eleanor found she was grateful. She was afraid that if she stopped or stared for too long at any one thing, in any of the many beautiful rooms they hurried past, she'd be mesmerized for days. "It was an oversight."

Eleanor doubted that, for some reason. Or she doubted that this woman made any oversights, perhaps. But this was her first day, and she had the distinct impression she'd already irritated her employer, so there was no reason to dig that ditch any deeper.

"I had a lovely walk," she said instead. "It was a nice chance to take in the area. And quite atmospheric."

"The moors are nothing if not filled with atmosphere," the housekeeper said, an undercurrent in her voice that made Eleanor's ears prick up. "You'll want to be careful of the winds, however. They crop up out of nowhere and howl terribly wherever they go. They have a way of getting under your skin, you'll find. Whether you're aware of it or not."

Eleanor didn't think Mrs. Redding was talking about the Yorkshire wind. Or not only about the Yorkshire wind.

"I'll be certain to dress appropriately for the elements, then," Eleanor said after a moment, her tone even.

The woman led her down an endless hallway, then stopped at the far end.

"These are your rooms," Mrs. Redding said, waving Eleanor into the waiting suite. "I hope it will be sufficient. I'm afraid it's a bit less spacious than some of the previous governesses were hoping for."

Eleanor wanted to tell the woman she had been expecting a closet, or perhaps a cot down in a basement. Wherever the servants were kept in a place like this.

But she couldn't get the words out of her mouth, because she was too busy being overwhelmed. Again.

Mrs. Redding had said *rooms* not *room*, and she hadn't misspoken.

The flat she shared with Vivi could easily have fit into one part of the large room she walked into first, and it took her long, stunned moments to realize that it was, in fact, her own sitting room. And Mrs. Redding was still going, straight into the next room, which it took Eleanor another long beat to realize was a great closet. For the grand wardrobe she didn't possess.

The bedroom itself was on the far side of a huge bathroom that looked like a spa to Eleanor's untutored eyes, and as she walked into it, trailing behind Mrs. Redding, Eleanor was certain that this was the biggest dwelling space she'd ever been in.

One side of the room was dominated by a massive four-poster bed with carved wood posts and more carved wood as a canopy over top, like some kind of queen's bower. There was another fireplace, and more places to sit around it, as if the whole sitting room wasn't enough.

Eleanor's breathing had gone a bit shallow. But she pulled it together, and smiled serenely at Mrs. Redding.

"It will do," she murmured, trying her best to sound dry and sophisticated and professional. Instead of like an overexcited child in a candy store.

After the older woman left her, with instructions about where and when Eleanor was to present herself later for a tour and a breakdown of her duties, Eleanor found herself standing in the middle of this bedroom she couldn't imagine ever calling her own. If possible, she felt more out of place than she had downstairs, where somehow the Duke's arrogance had made her forget herself and Geraldine's fierce, obvious loneliness had caught at her.

But here in these sumptuous rooms, she had nothing to fight. No one to defend. Only elegant emptiness all around.

Nothing but herself.

Whoever the hell that was.

CHAPTER THREE

HUGO HAD NO idea what had gotten into him.

He didn't know what it was about starchy, overly puffy-coated Eleanor Andrews that scraped beneath his skin. But there was no denying the fact that he, Hugo Grovesmoor, who had never chased a woman in his entire life, had been *lying in wait* for this one.

It was extraordinary.

Hugo told himself he needed to see what on earth was hidden beneath that enormous coat of hers, that was all. That not knowing might keep him up at night. Was she a marshmallow creature like the monster in that old movie? Or had she hid her true, svelte form away in a billowy suit of armor?

And he knew when she didn't back down in the foyer or unzip that great horror of a coat more than an inch or two that he needed to retreat back to his part of the house, carry on living the life of ease and leisure and loathing the whole of the world begrudged him these days, and forget all about his ward and the governess she'd decided to favor on sight. He knew it.

So he had no explanation for why he found himself lurking about in the wing he'd given over to Geraldine because he knew Mrs. Redding was giving Eleanor a tour and showing her where and how she'd be expected to do her work. The governess's quarters were in this same wing, one floor above, right up the nearby stairs—a fact that there was absolutely no reason at all for Hugo to keep reciting to himself.

"I didn't expect to see you, Your Grace," Mrs. Redding said when she swept out of the nursery that was now a playroom and found Hugo inspecting the rather horrifying paintings hanging on the walls in the hall that he remembered from his own childhood.

"I can't imagine why not, Mrs. Redding." Hugo kept studying the garish painting in front of him as he spoke. "I do own the house and am known to be in residence. Surely I could be expected to turn up sooner or later."

"In the child's wing? Unlikely." The older woman could still manage to infuse every syllable with genteel condemnation. A true skill, he'd always thought. "And yet here you are."

Hugo turned then, smiling faintly at Mrs. Redding as he looked behind her to where Eleanor stood.

And he understood in an instant that he'd made a terrible mistake.

Because Eleanor was not as puffy and large as her coat had suggested. Nor was she as whipcord-skinny as a gazelle's thigh, as many of her predecessors had been, eyes gleaming with avarice and ambition.

Quite the opposite, god help him.

The damned woman had the body of a goddess. A naughty fertility goddess. Eleanor had lush hips and generous breasts, sweetly separated by a tiny waist that made him hunger to test the span of it with his own hands. She was dressed in a perfectly conservative and appropriately opaque blouse over sensible trousers with a cardigan tossed on besides, and she still looked like an old pinup model. Her body was so markedly opulent that it made her harshly scraped back hair all the more intriguing—in that Hugo wanted to get his hands in it. Or feel it all over his naked body while she was engaged in other things, none of them involving any sort of harsh scraping at all.

Hugo knew he needed to stop. Now.

He needed to turn around this minute and get himself away from her, especially when she frowned at him from behind Mrs. Redding, and from beneath that fringe of hers. The legions of other women who had come this house and tried it on with him had pouted at him. They'd simpered and giggled. They'd made eyes at him over his ward's head and had dressed in preposterously inappropriate clothing while supposedly out taking walks on the grounds in the middle of rainstorms in the hope of attracting his notice.

Eleanor Andrews, on the other hand, barreled about in the ugliest coat he'd ever beheld in his life as if she didn't care whether or not she was found attractive, made no secret of the fact she held Hugo in rather low regard, and aimed disapproving frowns at him while she stood on his property as if she didn't expect to receive her salary from his accounts.

It was almost as if she didn't want anything from him.

That notion was so revolutionary it shook him a little. He found himself very nearly frowning himself, but caught it just in time. Hugo Grovesmoor did not *frown*. That might indicate he had thoughts, and that would never do. He was considered nothing more than a vessel of pointless and predatory evil, sent to earth to ruin every good thing in it at will.

He'd learned his place a long time ago.

And yet, "I'll finish giving Miss Andrews her tour of the premises," he heard himself say.

And then wondered if the rest of his admittedly impure thoughts were being broadcast on his face when both women stood there staring back at him. Then again, that was the benefit of owning half of England, wasn't it? He could bloody well do as he liked.

"Was I unclear?" he asked softly.

Mrs. Redding huffed slightly at that, but excused herself in the next moment because bristle as she might, the woman knew her place. And that left Hugo exactly where he shouldn't be, under any circumstances. Alone with Eleanor.

His ward's latest governess who happened to have the kind of body that made him feel like an adolescent boy all over again, all cock and delicious promise.

"How remarkably kind of you to take time out of

your busy schedule to welcome a lowly member of your staff, Your Grace," Eleanor said as Mrs. Redding's steps faded away, down the stairs and off into the busier parts of the house. Leaving them alone with nothing but the wind outside and the far-off sounds of Geraldine at her dinner on the other end of this hall, chattering away with her usual brace of nannies. "When I assume you must have any number of urgent ducal matters that require your attention."

"Dozens at every moment," Hugo agreed cheerfully, when what he actually had was the good sense to hire excellent people to handle such things. "And yet here I am, ready to wait on you hand and foot like a good host."

She smiled. It was a frozen sort of smile that shouldn't have hit him like that. Like a lick of heat in the place he was entirely too hard already.

"But I am not a guest, Your Grace," Eleanor said stiffly, as if he'd insulted her by suggesting otherwise.

"I'm certain I heard explicit criticism regarding my hospitality, did I not? Outside, when there was some question as to whether or not you were poaching from the estate?"

"There was never any real question about whether or not I was poaching, surely."

"And yet I felt as if I had many questions, none of which were answered. And many more of which were complicated by your performance in my foyer."

She made no apparent attempt to keep herself

from frowning at him all the more furiously. "My 'performance'?"

Hugo waited, brows raised expectantly, and her frown deepened.

"Your Grace," she managed to get out, sounding even stiffer than before.

Hugo tried as hard as he could to keep his mind free of any thoughts about Geraldine. Lest they stray from the girl he'd been called upon to care for, and end up on her mother instead.

And the less he thought about Isobel, the better.

The less anyone thought about Isobel, the better, in his opinion. Not that anyone had asked Hugo's opinion on Isobel in quite some time.

But as was to be expected, thoughts of Isobel and the damage she'd done—and still did despite the fact she was dead and buried—only made him angrier.

Not that he was angry, of course.

Hugo Grovesmoor was never *angry*. Angry was for people who had emotions, and it had been established long ago that he lacked that particular human frailty. In every paper possible. Over and over again.

"I don't know what else to call it but a performance." He felt his gaze go narrow. "Perhaps you can explain to me why you gave a little girl such false hope. Is that your angle?"

"Geraldine is a lovely young girl," Eleanor said in her prim way that made Hugo feel more of the sorts of things he was famous for never, ever feeling. In a great mad rush that made his fingers itch to touch her. "She does seem lonely and a bit lost, if I'm honest." Eleanor's startling gaze, frank and sturdy on his, made an interesting sort of heat pool inside of him. Hugo didn't like it. But not liking it, it turned out, didn't make it go away. "I look forward to being able to help her in some way. Assuming, of course, I'm allowed to do that."

"Do you imagine I would prevent you from doing the job for which I hired you in the first place? You have the most curious notions, Miss Andrews. Quite a fanciful imagination, it appears. Are you entirely certain that you are the best choice for a little girl you consider lost and lonely?"

The unfathomable woman shrugged as if it was no matter. "Whether I'm a good choice or bad choice, it appears I'm the only governess here."

"A circumstance that could change in an instant. On a whim. My whim."

Another shrug. "There's nothing I can do to control your whims, Your Grace. Is there? Best to muddle along and hope for the best, I think."

"The best being today's display? Telling a vulnerable child you'll always be her friend before you've taken off your coat or unpacked? Without knowing if she even likes you?" He shook his head. "Most women in your position play their games with me, Miss Andrews. They tend to leave the girl alone."

She stood there in her frumpy little outfit that should have made her look dumpy and instead made him think that he'd never seen a woman more magnetic. Especially since she didn't seem to be the least bit aware of it.

"All the more reason that someone ought to pay attention to the poor thing," she said briskly. "She's thirsty for a little companionship, clearly."

Eleanor was still eyeing him as if he was something distinctly unsavory as she spoke. And there was absolutely nothing new about that look. Hugo had seen that particular expression on more faces than he could begin to count. Friends, family members—or what few of each remained, anyway—and strangers on the street alike. He wasn't usually a receptacle for friendly glances, a fact of his existence he'd become inured to long since.

But for some reason, seeing that same old look on this woman's face dug into him. As if that *you are judged and found wanting* gaze she kept trained on him was attached to a sharp implement and she was raking it over his skin, if not jabbing it straight into his gut.

"Why do you want this job?" He didn't know why he bothered asking when he already knew. There were two reasons women applied for this position and Eleanor clearly wasn't thinking she'd angle her way into bed, which was a crying shame any way he looked at it. That left the money.

"Why wouldn't I want this job?" she asked, very coolly, in reply. "Fourteen other women had this job before me. It's obviously very popular."

"That's not an answer. And I can actually tell the difference between an answer and a nonanswer, which I accept may come as something of a surprise to you." He smiled at her, and made sure to show all his teeth. "I'm not just a pretty face, Miss Andrews."

If possible, her frown darkened even further. "I'm not following this conversation at all. Have you decided, now that I've actually moved into this house and have already met your ward, that it might be a good time to conduct a personal interview?"

"And if I am?"

"I think it's a little late. Don't you?"

"And I think, unless I'm very much mistaken or have succumbed to death without my knowledge—which should make this conversation significantly more upsetting than you seem to find it at present—that I am your employer. Or am I lost in some kind of dread fever dream, imagining myself the Duke of Grovesmoor?"

Hugo didn't know exactly when he realized he'd moved a little too close to her. Or perhaps she'd moved to close to him, he couldn't tell. All he knew was that they were no longer standing across from each other on different sides of the wide hallway. Instead they'd somehow closed the distance, and had met in the middle now.

Entirely too close to each other for Hugo's peace of mind, or whatever passed for that state. Because when he was closer to her, he was even more fascinated by her. He'd entertained the notion that it was the novelty of that hideous coat she'd worn earlier that had intrigued him, but no. He was still intrigued now.

More so.

The goddess curves didn't exactly help the situation, especially when she put her hands on her hips, which only made her lush figure that much more impossible to ignore.

"I don't know if you're imagining it or not," Eleanor said in a tone that only just managed to qualify as polite, "but if you're not the Duke of Grovesmoor, you've certainly managed to take on an identity with a remarkable amount of baggage."

Even that little swipe at his history intrigued him, because it was so direct. She was unlike any woman he'd ever encountered, even without that eyesore of a coat. It was something about the way she stood, wholly unimpressed and unintimidated by him, hands on her hips and her brown gaze utterly clear of any attempt at feminine wiles. It was the belligerent tilt of her jaw and the way she was clearly endeavoring to look down her nose at him from beneath her razor-sharp fringe. He imagined she did the same with her charges when they got uppity, and it didn't seem to matter to her that she was much shorter than he was.

And Hugo realized in that moment that he was perfectly content with being hated. He was used to being the focus of any number of dark feelings, vicious rumors, and random character assassinations. But he wasn't used to outright defiance. And certainly not to his face. For a man who had always considered himself entirely too modern for his circumstances, Hugo found that there was more than a little Ancient Duke in him than he'd ever imagined before. Because he wanted to pull rank. Badly.

Except it was more than that. He didn't want to crush *her*. The truth was, this woman made him *hungry*.

Hugo wanted a taste of her so badly that he could feel the need of it marching inside of him, as if his body was staging a full-scale mutiny. He didn't think he'd ever felt anything like it in his life. Hell. He knew he hadn't.

He was ravenous.

"I would suggest, Miss Andrews," he said, very carefully and very deliberately, and he kept his damned hands to himself despite the fact it took a Herculean application of self-will, "that you endeavor to recall which one of us is the Duke and which one the governess."

If Hugo expected her to be cowed by that, he was in for a surprise.

"I am not likely to forget that anytime soon," Eleanor replied without appearing to take even a moment to pause or rethink a thing. Not her belligerence or the way she stood there and took him on, exactly as she had outside. And certainly not her position— here in this house, much less here, in his grasp. "I was promised very little interaction with the owner of the house, Your Grace. That you were not available, ever, was made abundantly clear in all of the interviews."

"Most of the enterprising women who apply for the position want to see me, Miss Andrews. You must realize that it's the primary reason they condescend to grace these halls with their presence. And the primary reason they are sacked shortly thereafter."

She tilted her head slightly to one side. "And what did they do to get sacked?"

"I will leave that to your imagination."

"Did you chase all of them down on the grounds of the estate, charging about on a great big horse?"

He almost laughed at that. And it might have been that which floored him the most.

"And I ask again, why do you want this job? Because you don't seem to understand the usual boundaries that govern a woman in your position. Or have the faintest sense of self-preservation."

"I beg your pardon, Your Grace," she said in that same brisk tone, as if she thought she was managing him. As if both he and Geraldine were under her care, and he was the more difficult one by far. "All I'd like to do is start working. There's a little girl having her tea at the other end of this hall and it would be nice to get to know her a bit before our lessons start. If there isn't anything else…?"

"I am the boss, Miss Andrews," he reminded her. From between his teeth. "You are the employee. Everything about the way you are speaking to me is disrespectful, not to mention foolish. Why would you try to antagonize the person who pays your spectacularly generous salary?"

Her frown smoothed out a bit, though she didn't precisely soften. And still, Hugo wanted to taste that faint crease between her brows, where the edge of her fringe kissed her skin the way he wanted to do.

"In point of fact, I won't be paid for two weeks," she said after a moment, as if she couldn't help herself. Maybe she really couldn't.

He couldn't have said why that notion washed through him like a new sort of heat.

"A notable distinction," Hugo murmured.

And then, because he loved nothing more than complicating any given situation beyond repair, the better to make it worse, he kissed her.

They were standing so close that it seemed almost impossible to avoid for another second. Maybe that was his excuse. He slid his palm over her cheek, marveling at the sensation of such sweet, silken skin beneath his hand despite how severely she'd been regarding him all this time, and then it was the easiest thing in the world to hold her fast and claim her mouth with his.

And then they were in real trouble, because she tasted like magic.

CHAPTER FOUR

ELEANOR HAD NO idea what was happening.

He was kissing her.

Hugo was *kissing* her. The hated Duke of Grovesmoor himself had his *mouth* on hers.

And nothing about that was all right. It was dangerous and it was terrible and it was shocking—

But even worse, she liked it.

She more than liked it.

There were no words—and least none she knew—that could begin to describe how much she liked it.

It was like fire. It was an explosion, and only the fact that he was holding her against him kept her from shattering into a million pieces, she was sure of it.

What Eleanor knew about kissing could be summed up in two very short words: not much. But the single adolescent fumbling she'd subjected herself to at a mortifying school disco years and years ago bore no resemblance to this.

Hugo's mouth on hers was untroubled, somehow. Unhurried. He sampled her lips as if he planned to keep on doing so for hours. Days, perhaps. He seemed entirely and wholly unrushed, teasing her and tasting her, then licking his way inside to do it all over again.

With a devastating thoroughness that made her tremble. Everywhere.

And she didn't know what was worse, that mouth of his licking fire into her in ways she could hardly begin to process, or the heat of his hand as he held her face to his. Her cheek felt as if it had been branded, as if he was still pressing a red-hot iron to her skin, but for some reason she had no desire whatsoever to step away.

And still he kissed her.

As if a kiss was not a finite thing, a buss on the cheek or halfhearted peck, easily given and more easily forgotten. A real kiss—because Eleanor had no doubt that what Hugo was doing to her was the real thing, something she'd had no idea even existed all this time—was more of a slow burn.

It was longing made physical, then slowly kindled into an ache.

And oh, how Eleanor ached.

She didn't know how she'd ended up standing so close to him in the first place. She'd told herself repeatedly to keep her distance from the man, because no good could possibly come of their proximity when she was so *aware* of him, and then there she was. Stood in the center of the hallway with her hands on her hips as if she'd half a mind to scold the man, or as if she'd forgotten herself completely and was dressing down *the Duke*. Eleanor had no idea what had come over her. It was like an out-of-body experience. As if she was being haunted by some stroppy, mouthy ghost that was taking her over and making her act as if she very much wanted to be fired on her very first day...

She hadn't the slightest idea what she thought she was doing.

And now this.

Whatever *this* was, that was setting her on fire and tearing her apart at once.

But then it hit her, as his impossibly addictive mouth moved on hers, making her feel as if a lightning flash had been trapped between them. This was Hugo Grovesmoor. *This was what he did.* She hadn't expected him to be as articulate as he was, it was true. She'd expected his dark good looks to seem seedy and tatty in person—and she'd imagined she'd barely see him. But it occurred to her that she should have expected this kind of thing from him.

Hugo was a man who was willing to use his body to get what he wanted. Anything he wanted. Particularly if it was harmful to others. How could Eleanor have let herself forget? The fact that his kiss felt like a revelation was something that should have filled her with shame.

It would, she was certain, just as soon as she had time to collect herself.

Somewhere that lightning wasn't burning her alive.

Eleanor pushed at his chest, and that was problematic too, because he appeared to be made of more of that iron. Worse, he was much too hot beneath that soft T-shirt, and she had no desire whatsoever to let go.

No matter how she knew she should.

Lazily, taking his time, Hugo raised his head. His whiskey-colored eyes gleamed as he gazed down at her and Eleanor could feel that, too. She could feel so many things she thought she might collapse. Part of her wanted nothing more than to let all that emotion take her straight down to the floor, but she was made of sterner stuff. She'd had to be. She had Vivi to think about.

"Is this why all fourteen previous governesses left?" Eleanor demanded, and she was horrified to hear her voice shake. "Is this a test?" She swallowed, hard. "Geraldine is only just down the hall."

Something flashed in those dark eyes of his, but he dropped his hand. And Eleanor told herself that what rushed in her then was relief. Triumph. Not something a great deal more like loss.

She could feel the way he kissed her everywhere, in ways that made no sense. There was a twisting, melting ball of sensation deep in her belly. There was a rawness in her chest. Her breasts felt weighted, heavy. And there was a dampness behind her eyes that she knew perfectly well was too complicated to be simple tears.

"I enjoy nothing more than living down to each and every one of a person's low expectations of me, of course," Hugo said in that mocking, cut-glass way of his. "Do you not find me entertaining, Miss Andrews? Could there be anything more delightful than to discover I am exactly as you imagined I'd be? Depraved and indifferent and thoroughly spoiled, inside and out?"

Eleanor had been thinking along those lines herself, but somehow, hearing him say it all out loud like that—with such bitterness, and something she could have sworn bordered despair—made something inside of her turn over.

But she shoved it aside, because none of this should have happened. Not with her. She wasn't the sort of woman men grabbed and kissed in spontaneous bursts of passion. That was Vivi's life. Her sister was forever fending off male attention wherever she went. That was how Eleanor knew that there was no reason for a man like Hugo to put his hands on her unless that was just something he did as a matter of course, the way the tabloids had always claimed—or if he was making fun of her, somehow.

She'd never heard of mockery by kiss, but what did she know? She'd spent her life working rather than socializing, and she'd never bloomed into a needy curiosity of the opposite sex the way everyone had claimed she would. Something that made her profoundly grateful, as what she didn't need or even wonder about, she couldn't miss.

"I think it's best if we pretend this never happened," she said, as evenly as she could, pleased to find she'd managed to strip the tremor from her voice.

Hugo regarded her from the near foot of height

he had on her, and the fact he was dressed so casually, she realized, did nothing to take away from that matter-of-fact power he seemed to exude even so. How had she not noticed that before?

Because he hides it, a voice from deep inside of her replied with far too much authority. *In the same way you lie to yourself about the things you need.*

Eleanor didn't like that at all. She ignored it.

"That will make it difficult, you understand, to sell your salacious story to the tabloids," Hugo was saying in a cold sort of tone, as if he was discussing something that wouldn't affect him one way or the other.

"I couldn't do that if I wanted to, which I don't." Eleanor thought her voice softened at the end there, so she tried to even it out again. She put her spine into it. "I signed an extremely comprehensive nondisclosure agreement, Your Grace. Surely you must be aware of it."

"What I am aware of is that the penalty for breaking that nondisclosure agreement is a certain amount of pounds sterling. Should the tabloids offer, say, twice that amount, it might well be worth it to break the agreement. To a certain type of person, of course."

"I..." Eleanor very rarely found herself a loss for words. She didn't understand the sensation warring inside of her. That strange longing, or the fact she had to curl her hands into fists at her side to keep them to herself. She, who was not the sort of person who liked to touch others or even to be touched herself.

She, who had never had to fight *not* to touch someone in her life. She was baffled. "I would never do that."

"Because you are such a good person, naturally. My mistake."

His sardonic tone could have stripped the paint from the walls and Eleanor nearly checked to see if it had. But didn't, because she could feel her reaction in the flush that heated her cheeks, and she thought that was more than enough of a response.

"Because who would do that?" she asked, almost helplessly.

The expression on the Duke's face was all razor-sharp amusement, but all Eleanor could feel in the space between them was more of that same bitterness that cut a little too close to despair. Dark and thick and everywhere.

Hopeless, she thought, and didn't know why that made her ache again, the way she had when he'd kissed her. Only sharper.

"Everyone has their price, I assure you," Hugo said quietly.

As if he was making a prediction. A terrible one.

"Do you?" Eleanor dared to ask.

The expression on his face then made her heart kick at her, then sink into that same sharp ache. But his laugh was worse, dark enough to fill the hall, if not the grand house arrayed all around them, too.

"Especially me, Miss Andrews," he told her, almost gently. Though his dark eyes blazed, and were anything but gentle. Anything but soft. "Me most of all."

* * *

Eleanor woke in a room fit for a princess and told herself that the unsettling scene in the hallway that had kept her awake and that kiss that had invaded her dreams hadn't happened.

Because surely she could not possibly have been so stupid as to go full *Jane Eyre* on the very first day of her new job, within hours of meeting the Duke and his ward. Before she'd even unpacked her case or figured out what her new job actually entailed. Eleanor had never been that kind of silly. She'd never had the time or, if she was honest, the inclination to fling herself headlong into the sort of mad passions and silly entanglements the bright young things all around her seemed to flock to so mindlessly, like moths to a wholly avoidable flame.

Until last night, Eleanor would have confidently asserted that she simply didn't have those sorts of feelings or bodily reactions. That she wasn't wired that way.

She decided she would treat that kiss as if it hadn't happened, because it shouldn't have. And because she had no idea how to handle all the things she *felt*. As if she was a moth battering itself against a light after all.

But she soon found that it didn't matter how she handled what should never have happened, because the Duke was nowhere to be found over the next few weeks.

Eleanor told herself that was a good thing.

Geraldine was a bright, often funny kid, and even

on her less than stellar days, it was far more interesting to work with her than it was to answer ringing phones and take the odd bit of abuse from walk-ins and disgruntled clients and snarky deliverymen. Far better Geraldine than her last immediate supervisor, Eleanor thought more than once.

"I feel terrible that I pushed you into taking this strange job," Vivi told her a few days into her time at Groves House.

"It's actually a good fit, believe it or not. I like it."

Vivi plowed right on, her voice merry and sharp. "I bullied you into it and now you're trapped in the bowels of Yorkshire in some moldering old stack of stones."

Eleanor was sunk deep into her luxurious bathtub, bubbles high and the hot water silky against her skin. She had a book on her little bath tray, a glass of wine and some fine cheese she'd never tasted before, and a fire crackling in the other room. She and Geraldine had spent the day investigating the sciences and giggling uproariously for no particular reason, until Eleanor had delivered her to the nannies who supervised the little girl's tea and bedtime.

"The poor tyke can't go to a proper school, can she?" the slightly friendlier of the two notably unfriendly nannies had said out in the hall after Geraldine had run into her rooms, as if Eleanor had argued otherwise. "Those worthless journos won't leave her alone for a minute. If I knew who sold them stories about the Duke I'd give them a piece of my mind, believe me."

As if Hugo was a good man who merited that kind of defense.

The other woman had huffed off after Geraldine. Leaving Eleanor finished with lessons—and thus finished with her work for the day—at four-thirty. Which was late, as they were usually finished hours sooner unless they'd taken a little trip further afield.

Eleanor had never had such easy, comfortable hours.

But for some reason, she didn't tell Vivi any of that, and not only because that sharp merriment in her voice suggested her sister had been tossing back spirits.

"I'm fine, really," Eleanor said instead, like a proper martyr.

And felt terrible about herself as Vivi mouthed a few more drunken apologies, then rang off.

But not terrible enough to correct her sister's impression that she was muddling through dire circumstances in their next conversation. Or the next. Or, for that matter, let Vivi know that she had in fact met the disgraced Duke himself. More than "met" him.

She told herself that because that kiss had been such an egregious misstep, and because the Duke had disappeared thereafter, it hadn't happened. So there was no need to tell Vivi about it, as her sister would only leap to the wrong conclusions.

But something deep inside her whispered a different, darker reason.

Eleanor ignored that, too.

The truth was that Eleanor had wanted to become

a teacher years ago, but hadn't thought she could make enough money at it to serve Vivi's purposes and hers—and certainly not without heading back to school to get the proper certification. There had obviously been no time for that. *I can only be dazzling for a few years, after all,* Vivi would say. Working with Geraldine was a lot like fulfilling an old dream. It was like a little glance down the road not taken, which, Eleanor found, she liked as much—if not more—than the one she'd been on all this time.

And with her focus on Geraldine and the new lessons she plotted out every night on her laptop, she hardly noticed the absence of the Duke.

Until she fell asleep, that was, when that kiss haunted her dreams.

And Eleanor woke each morning flustered and red-faced, and entirely too warm. Because in her dreams, vivid and wild, they didn't stop at a single kiss.

CHAPTER FIVE

"HIS GRACE WILL not be returning from Spain today as planned," Mrs. Redding announced one morning, when Eleanor had dropped by the housekeeper's office off the kitchens to go over Geraldine's schedule of excursions so the cook and staff could be kept informed.

Eleanor blinked. "Oh?"

Later, Eleanor thought immediately, she'd be furious with herself for sounding something other than blandly disinterested. But all she could do now was gaze back at the disapproving older woman and pretend she hadn't sounded a little too intrigued.

Maybe more than a little. She hated herself for that, too.

"We expected him in residence today," Mrs. Redding said matter-of-factly, very much as if she hadn't heard anything in Eleanor's voice. Eleanor told herself that *of course* she hadn't. It was all in her head, because Eleanor was the one wandering around with the guilty conscience—and the memory of that kiss. Not Mrs. Redding. She hoped. "But his plans have changed, and he will be making a brief trip to Dublin before returning."

"I didn't realize he wasn't in residence now," Eleanor lied, her voice as bland as she could make it. She punctuated it by taking a calm sip of her tea.

Mrs. Redding eyed her as if she knew the tea was a prop. "When the Duke is in residence, he likes to have Geraldine presented to him at least every other week at dinner. By the child's current governess, so he can assess both Geraldine's and the governess's progress."

"Well, I suppose that explains why the Duke has appeared so hands-off since I arrived." Eleanor managed a laugh. "I thought perhaps he didn't have much interest in his ward."

The temperature in the room seemed to plummet at that. Eleanor watched Mrs. Redding's gaze frost over right there before her.

"It would be wiser to put a little less stock in what people say about His Grace from afar," the housekeeper said, as if each syllable cut the roof of her mouth on the way out. "That tabloid creation bears no resemblance to the man I've known since he was a child. A man who took in an orphaned child out of the goodness of his heart and is still painted a villain for it."

Eleanor took her time placing her cup of tea back in its saucer, surprised at the vehemence in the older woman's voice.

"Having a ward thrust upon one and being expected to raise them must be something of an adjustment," she said after a moment.

Mrs. Redding shifted behind her desk, and gazed at Eleanor for a moment over the top of her eyeglasses.

"We are a mite protective of the Duke here," she said with the same quiet intensity, and Eleanor couldn't tell if that was a warning or an explanation. "It's a rare stranger indeed who has his best interests at heart. He has been so long in that spotlight that the spotlight is all anyone sees, but we see the boy who grew up here." Her gaze edged back into chilly territory. "The whole of England might be dedicated to telling nasty stories about His Grace, but they are never told here. Ever."

Eleanor couldn't help feeling as if she'd been slapped again. And harder, this time. As if the fact no one had met her at the train station when she'd arrived had been a test, not an oversight. She wanted to ask Mrs. Redding directly but didn't quite dare.

It was the same with all the staff in Groves House, she found as the days passed and the weather grew more blustery and grim. Each day was bleaker than the one before. The trees grew ever more stark and the rain fell colder. Icier. And the other members of the household were as uninterested in Eleanor's presence weeks into her residence as they'd been at the start. She ended up eating her meals alone in her own rooms because when she entered the common staff areas, all conversation stopped, which did not exactly aid the digestion.

"What do you mean they're all offish?" Vivi asked in one of their phone calls. She sounded distant and preoccupied, the way she often did when Eleanor called her instead of the other way around. As if she had her mobile clamped to her shoulder while she bustled about doing other things. Much more important things, her distracted tone suggested.

Eleanor told herself, brusquely, that it wasn't entirely fair to attach meaning to Vivi's *tone*. They each played their parts, after all. If she had a problem with that, she'd had years to say so. She could have objected years ago when their reluctant, distantly related cousin had eyed the pair of them as adolescents and set the course of their lives.

"Might as well marry a rich man as a poor man," she'd tutted at them one afternoon. *"You two have nothing in this world but Vivi's pretty face. I'd use it to better yourselves, if I were you."*

"I mean exactly that." Eleanor said now, scowling at the memory. As if Vivi hadn't already been a miracle, walking the way she had when the doctors thought she never would. And it wasn't entirely true that all they had was Vivi's face, was it? Because what was Vivi's face without Eleanor's financial wizardry and prowess with a sewing needle? "They're a closed group. No newcomers."

Eleanor had taken to walking in the evenings and tonight she'd taken the back stairs that led from the kitchen into a wing she never been in before. She'd climbed up to the second floor and found herself in a long hallway that doubled as an art gallery. Obvious, recognizable masterpieces worth billions were flung on walls next to what looked like very dour and period-appropriate versions of Hugo. But she concentrated on her phone call, not the wigs and funny hats and companion animals in the portraits before her.

Vivi sighed, which definitely put Eleanor's back up, and no matter that she tried to pretend otherwise. "Are you there to make friends, Eleanor?"

"Of course not." She could hear the tension in her voice, and forced herself to take a breath. "I know why I'm here, Vivi. All I'm saying is that it wouldn't be the worst thing to have a friendly face about the place. That's all."

Vivi, clearly no longer feeling guilty or bullying or drunk, sighed again.

"Don't go moping about the place. No one likes an Eeyore."

Eleanor found she was scowling at the painting in front of her, biting her tongue. As in, literally pressing it against her teeth to keep from saying something back in the same dismissive tone.

"I should think you ought to feel grateful that you're not required to work so hard for the friendship of people you won't know in a year's time," Vivi said dismissively.

It hadn't really occurred to Eleanor to think about the people here—or her position here or whole solitary little life here, really—as temporary. But of course it was. Even if all went well, a girl only needed a governess for so long.

"I think I have a few years before I can happily drift off into the sunset," she pointed out, and she was proud of herself for sounding as if she was smiling, not scowling. "Geraldine is seven, not seventeen."

Vivi laughed. "You're not disappearing into the north forever, Eleanor. You're supposed to make us enough to cover our bills and then come back."

"I didn't realize that was the plan. Especially when the longer I stay, the more I'll make."

"Eleanor, please," Vivi said, her tone light. But there was something beneath it that wedged its way into Eleanor's stomach and sat there. Heavily. "I can't possibly do all this without you. You're on holiday, nothing more."

Eleanor finished off the call, and found herself staring blankly out one of the windows in this strange art gallery hall, her stomach still not quite right. Because it was tempting to pretend that Vivi couldn't do without her emotionally, that she missed Eleanor herself, but deep down, Eleanor suspected that wasn't true. Just yesterday Vivi had been in a panic about how to pay all the bills and get the rent in, and she'd moaned something about what a tip the flat was since there was no one to tidy it up.

Because, of course, the person who usually handled all those things was Eleanor.

It was a good thing Vivi thought Eleanor was suffering in a pile of debris in the middle of a moor. Because if her sister had any idea how luxurious Eleanor's lifestyle was at present, Eleanor had no doubt Vivi would contrive a way to get herself up to Groves House so she could enjoy it herself.

And Eleanor was obviously far more deeply selfish than she'd ever imagined, because for once in her life, she didn't want to share something with the sister she'd always loved to the point of distraction.

She stuck her mobile in the pocket of the black trousers she wore and moved over to the windows. The gallery was set up over the back of the house and looked out over the tangle of the back gardens that led straight into the brooding moors. There was a full moon tonight, tossing a spooky sort of silvery light here and there, silently moving in and out of the clouds, and making the whole of Yorkshire seem to gleam.

If gloomily.

Maybe it was because she was tucked away in this desolate old house. Maybe it was because the halls were always empty, the locals were unfriendly, and the nights were already starting to seem as if they lasted three times as long as the day. Maybe it was because she felt a bit too much like a gothic waiting to happen, locked away in here.

But when had she decided that she was so all right with being alone? Her goal had always been Vivi's great marriage. She'd never thought about what *she* would do once that happened.

She shivered as she thought about the Duke's mouth on hers, firm and commanding. And if the highlights of her circumscribed life were the potent, powerful dreams that shook through her every night, all featuring Hugo in searing detail, well. That was more than some people ever had. Maybe it was enough.

Eleanor took a deep breath and vowed it would be. It would have to be.

"Dare I hope that your unexpected appearance outside my private rooms is an invitation, Miss Andrews?"

Eleanor told herself she was hallucinating. Auditory hallucinations, which were really just another part of a regular old haunting, according to all the scary films she'd seen in her time.

She took her time turning to check. And it was worse than any run-of-the-mill haunting.

Hugo stood there at the other end of the long gallery. And this time, he looked exactly like a duke. Exactly like every fantasy Eleanor had ever had of a man that powerful, for that matter. He was dressed all in black and looked vaguely historical. It took her a shattering beat of her heart or two to realize it was because he wore a top hat that should have looked absurd over a long black cloak that did. Or anyway, should have. *Would have*, even, had another man worn it.

But Eleanor was very much afraid, as her throat went dry and her stomach twisted into something that wasn't quite anxiety, that there was nothing Hugo could do that was truly absurd. Now when he looked the way he did.

And certainly not when he was looking at her.

"You appear to be dressed as if you've been off

visiting Regency England," she said dryly. And only she had to know that the dryness in her mouth was more physical response to him than any attempt on her part to sound indifferent.

"Naturally," Hugo said, as if an agreement. "I've been out terrifying the tenants and topping barmaids in my stagecoach." He raised a brow. "Or possibly I was attending a Halloween party, complete with fancy dress. You must be aware that it's the end of October."

She was aware of almost nothing but him. That was the terrifying truth that seared its way through her then, making her entire body feel…different. As if there was a fire in her bones, and it was changing her. Or had already done so, dream by dream, without her realizing it.

Hugo moved toward her in that graceful way of his, as if he was half liquid. When he drew too close, Eleanor desperately wanted to think of something appropriately boring and dampening to say—but instead found that she still couldn't seem to think of anything at all but the sensation of his mouth on hers.

His gaze darkened, as if her thoughts were written all over her face, but if they were he didn't say a word. He only kept moving, brushing past her and indicating that she should follow him with nothing more than a supremely arrogant tilt of his chin. And yet Eleanor found herself obeying.

As if this was as close to happy as she was likely to get.

Hugo stopped at the door at the far end of the gallery and looked back over his shoulder.

"Come," he said, and Eleanor didn't know if she was tempted or terrified. Or some far more potent combination of both.

All she knew was that she picked up her pace, on command.

And Hugo's dangerous mouth curved. "Perhaps it's time I conducted that interview, after all."

Hugo felt like the big, bad wolf.

It was not exactly unpleasant. God knew he'd had nothing to do these past years save sharpen his fangs.

And the distance he'd put between him and this governess who shouldn't have tempted him hadn't dulled a thing. Not the impossible lushness of her curves or that tiny waist that mesmerized him. Not her apparent inability to cower before him like almost every other person he encountered in this house.

Above all, it had failed to dull his reaction to her.

He was hard and needy in an instant, and inviting her into his private library was only going to make it worse. He knew he shouldn't do it. He knew better than to tempt himself—because when had he ever resisted temptation?

But when his hand was on the door, she stopped, and she looked at him as if she was fighting her way out of a magic spell.

"I can't… Is that your bedroom?"

Hugo was merely a man. And not a good one.

It took everything he had not to throw her over his shoulder and carry her off to his actual bedroom.

"That tone of voice would be so much more effective if you were clutching a strand of pearls, I think," he said instead, like a bloody saint. Maybe that was why he sounded so gruff. "As it is, the offended virgin act needs a little bit of work."

Eleanor blinked, and straightened. "So I should take that as a yes, this is in fact your bedchamber."

There was no earthly reason why Hugo should be baring his teeth in a poor semblance of a smile, far too much wolf and very, very little of him—even that less than stellar man he usually was.

"If you are so eager to take to my bed, you need only ask. These games are so unbecoming, Miss Andrews. Do you not think?"

"Your Grace…"

But she didn't turn tail and run.

Hugo smirked at her, because it was that or touch her, and once he started he doubted he'd stop for at least a week. Maybe three. She'd haunted him across the planet, with her defiant gaze and her unimpressed mouth and all of her mouthwatering curves. He'd decided that if she was going to torture him, she might as well do it in person.

"Relax. This is my library. Not a den of iniquity." His lips twitched. "Depending, I suppose, on what books you choose to read."

He threw the door open and strode through. He did not look behind him to see if she followed because that, too, was tempting fate.

If she was walking away from him, he didn't know what he'd do.

The very thought appalled him. Who *hadn't* walked away from England's most reviled man? He welcomed it. He thrived on it. He certainly shouldn't care in the least what this governess did.

But once again, she followed him, and he was forced to admit he liked it. And that there was something else simmering in him when she shut the door behind her. It felt a bit too much like relief, though Hugo knew that couldn't be it. True villains felt nothing, through and through. They were made of stone and had no regrets.

Everybody said so.

He waved his hand at the comfortable leather chair before the crackling fire, and allowed himself a small, triumphant smile when she sat. Obediently. Despite that look in her dark eyes that suggested that at any moment, she might break for it.

Hugo told himself he wouldn't chase her if she did. Of course he wouldn't. But as he rid himself of the top hat and his great cloak, he wasn't entirely sure.

"I've been in the grand library downstairs," Eleanor said after the silence drew out. "This is built on a smaller scale, but is no less impressive."

"I'm delighted you think so. I did wonder."

She was looking at his books, not him, but he was sure he saw her lips move as if she was biting back a smile.

"Fat mysteries next to battered paperbacks," she

murmured, gazing around the room. "Ruminations on astral physics and—is that philosophy?—next to the entire series of Harry Potter books."

"Signed first editions, obviously."

"Careful," Eleanor said softly, still not looking at him. "Books tell a whole lot more about a person than the things they say. Or the things others say. Well-worn books tell all manner of inconvenient truths about their owners."

Something rushed through Hugo then, almost as if he was lightheaded. Or drunk.

Foreboding, he thought grimly.

As if, were she to look too closely at the truths his books told about him, she'd know what was real and what wasn't. And everything would change. *He* would change.

And Hugo was perfectly content to stay exactly as he was. Hated and all the more powerful for it. The more they made him into the bogeyman, the happier he was.

Because all those people who had bought Isobel's act deserved to imagine that the love child she'd made with that idiot Torquil was forced to pay for her parents' sins in the grip of a monster like him. They deserved to worry themselves sick about it, torturing themselves as they imagined scenes of neglect and abuse, because that was the least that could be expected from the villain Isobel had created.

"Every good story needs a villain, darling," she'd told him archly that first time.

That being the first time Hugo had woken to find

a version of himself he didn't recognize in the papers. The first time he'd had the sickening realization that the fake version was more believable. That even when he tried to clear his name or at least tell a different side to the story, no one wanted to hear it. Terrible Hugo was far more compelling than the real one ever could have been.

He remembered the time he'd tracked her down across the planet in Santa Barbara, California, to demand that she stop the insanity, years into her game. That she stop telling those lies. That she leave him out of the sick games she liked to play with people's lives—and not because it bothered him. He'd long passed the point where anything she did could bother him. But his father had still been alive then, and it had wrecked the old man.

"Hurting your lovely old father isn't my goal, of course," Isobel had murmured, out by one of those impossibly still and blue California pools, all hipbones and malice in a tiny bikini. She'd smiled at him over her oversized sunglasses. *"It's a happy bonus, that's all."*

"There is nothing you can do to me, Isobel," he'd told her fiercely then. *"You cannot take my heritage from me. You cannot siphon off a single penny of my fortune. Whether I am liked or I am hated, I will still become the Duke in due course. Grovesmoor will carry on. Don't you understand? I'm bulletproof."*

But she'd only laughed at him.

"And I'm a better storyteller," she'd said.

Hugo had borne the brunt of that damned story of

hers for years. He still did. But now he had his own weapon in the form of a child everyone assumed he hated and the world's endless censure.

And he had no intention of giving it up.

Certainly not to a governess with the body of a screen idol and too much uncertain temper in her dark eyes. A woman who looked for truth in his books and didn't know when to back down from a fight she couldn't win.

No matter how much he wanted her.

CHAPTER SIX

ELEANOR COULD ONLY stare at the Duke's book collection for so long before it became awkward. Or rather, a little too obvious that she was going out of her way to avoid looking at him directly.

She told herself she was simply appreciating the amount of literature he kept on his shelves and at hand at all times, that was all. The truth was she'd never lived in a place where she could keep more than her absolute most favorite books on what little shelf space she could spare. She wouldn't have minded spending a few hours getting lost in this place.

But, of course, her employer had not called her into his library to offer her the chance to browse.

Pull yourself together, Eleanor, she chided herself.

She sat on the edge of a buttery soft leather chair, afraid to let herself sink back into it. Afraid she'd never pull herself out again. But when she was finally sure that her expression was nothing but serene and dared to look at him again, everything had gotten much worse.

Much, much worse.

Because while Hugo had removed that top hat and cloak that made him look like something out of the sort of fantasies Eleanor had never had before coming to Groves House, Hugo in nothing but exquisitely fitted dark trousers and a white shirt that opened at the neck was infinitely more dangerous.

And tempting in all kinds of ways she'd never experienced before in her life.

She could feel each and every temptation as if it was a separate strand of heat, swirling around inside of her and making her feel like a stranger to herself.

Hugo moved from the great desk where he'd carelessly tossed his coat and hat, and stalked across the room toward her. Of course he wasn't *stalking*, Eleanor told herself sharply. The man was simply walking from one end of the library to the other. The way people did when they wished to cross a space.

There was no reason at all that she should find herself holding her breath the way she was. Or clenching tight every single muscle in her body as she perched on the edge of that heavy chair, until she thought she might snap in half.

Hugo dropped himself down into the leather chair across from hers. He did not exactly sit nicely. Instead, of course, he sprawled. He was bigger every time she looked at him, it seemed, and his solidly built body covered more than simply the chair. His legs were long and he thrust them out before him, eating up the thick rug that was all that sat between their chairs.

He wasn't simply *sitting there*, Eleanor thought, with a mounting sense of unease. He seemed to claim the entire room with that offhanded masculine grace of his. As if he was the hazard, not the fire, which crackled away beside them and yet seemed to dim everything that wasn't Hugo.

It would be a lot easier, Eleanor reflected with no little hysteria, if the man was as seedy and dissolute as he'd always seemed in the tabloids. Instead of finely chiseled everywhere and exuding entirely too much sheer, powerful certainty the way other men reeked of cologne.

"How fares my ward?" Hugo asked.

So politely, so mildly, that Eleanor thought she must have been imagining the strange currents that seemed to fill the room—and her—with such an odd, electric sensation. It was clearly her, she told herself sternly. She was the one who was having some kind of allergic reaction to being in this man's presence. Or perhaps it was all those centuries of Grovesmoor influence and authority that he wore so easily when he was meant to be nothing but a layabout. Eleanor supposed it could even be the broad span of his shoulders, entirely too sculpted and athletic for a man so famously devoted to his own leisure.

But when she met his gaze, she understood that she wasn't suffering from some allergy to the aristocracy. Or if she was, he was too. Because his dark eyes burned with a bright, intent fire Eleanor didn't recognize, but could feel. Everywhere.

"Geraldine is very well," she said before she forgot to respond. Which wouldn't do at all.

Thinking about the little girl was the way to survive this, clearly. Eleanor made her spine as much of a straight line she could bear without actually hurting herself, and folded her hands neatly in her lap. She found that if she gazed at Hugo's chin instead of directly into his overwhelming, challenging gaze, she could pretend to be looking at him without actually risking too much direct eye contact.

And that little disconnection made it possible for her to catch her breath. To keep her heart from beating entirely too fast. Or anyway, pretend that she had herself under control, which would have to be enough.

"She's quite intelligent. And funny, it turns out. Not all little girls are funny, of course." Eleanor felt herself flush slightly, because she sounded a great deal as if she was babbling. And she never babbled. "Not that I have vast experience with seven-year-old girls, but I was one."

Hugo looked boneless and hungry, and the combination made Eleanor's pulse dance.

"Some time ago, if I'm not mistaken," he said.

"A lady does not discuss her age, Your Grace."

"You're a governess, are you not? Not a lady in the classic sense, if you will excuse the pedantry. But more to the point, you're entirely too young to become missish and coy about your age. Surely that is the province of women significantly longer in the tooth than you."

Eleanor found she was meeting his gaze, and had no idea when she'd given up the chin offensive. It was a mistake. She felt as if she'd sat out in the sun too long and was now a miserable prickle everywhere she had skin.

"I'm twenty-seven, if that's what you're asking. And I hope that you're not asking that. Because that would be unpardonably rude."

Hugo's lips twitched. "The horror."

"And I'm surprised that a duke of England should bother himself to pull rank. Surely in the absence of a Windsor lurking about, that's a bit redundant."

"You cannot be surprised, Miss Andrews." The corner of Hugo's mouth tipped up, but if that was a smile, it was entirely too dark. "I have yet to encounter a single story ever told about me that did not make it clear I am the worst kind of person. A stain upon the nation."

"Are you suggesting that I believe everything I've read about you? My understanding—" culled entirely from books and television and supermarket checkout queues, which she did not plan to share with him "—was that most celebrities claim that the things that are written about them in places like the tabloids are lies."

Something in his expression shifted. Eleanor couldn't put her finger on it. It was as if he turned quietly to stone, everywhere, even as his gaze changed. Melted, she would have said, if she were the fanciful sort. Into a far more powerful spirit, more intense than his usual whiskey.

"And if I were to tell you that, indeed, nearly everything that has ever been written about me in the press is a lie, you would believe that?"

Hugo wasn't exactly smirking, but there was no mistaking the challenge he'd thrown at her or the way he lounged there in the chair opposite her while he did it. His oddly intent gaze was taut on hers while one long finger tapped the side of his jaw, rough now instead of clean-shaven.

He looked decadent. Sinful.

Eleanor had absolutely no trouble believing every wicked thing she'd ever heard about him. Ever.

And it did absolutely nothing to diminish his appeal.

"Your reputation precedes you, of course, Your Grace," she said briskly, fighting to keep her wits about her when she couldn't seem to pull in a full breath. "But it is not your reputation that concerns me. It is your ward's education."

"A clever dodge, Miss Andrews, but I'd prefer it if you answered the question."

Eleanor reminded herself that this was not a situation that required her honesty. This man was not interested in her frank opinion of him. How could he be? Hugo was the Duke of Grovesmoor. And her employer. If he wanted to pretend that the stories about him were lies, it was only in Eleanor's best interest to agree.

Because, as her sister reminded her almost every night, this was about the money. It was most certainly not about that odd weight in her chest that urged her to do the exact opposite of what she knew to be necessary. And smart.

She ignored that weight. She shoved it aside and pretended she couldn't feel it. She made herself smile. Politely.

"Everyone knows the tabloids are filled with lies," she murmured, hoping that placated him. "All smoke, no fire."

Hugo shook his head as if he were disappointed in her. "I believe you are lying, Miss Andrews, and I am shocked onto my soul." That curve in the corner of his mouth deepened. "And yes, I do have one. Clouded and murky though it may be."

It was entirely too easy to drift off, staring at this man in all his dark, threatening beauty, as if he was an approaching storm and the worst that could happen to her was that she'd get a bit wet. But she had to stop thinking of him that way. She had to do something about the strange signals her body sent off that made her entirely too nervous. That tightness in her breasts. The knotted thing in her belly. And that odd, melting sensation lower still.

She had to remember what she was doing here. It was about the money and it was about Geraldine, and all these strange electrical moments were distractions, nothing more.

Because of course they couldn't be anything more.

"I've given Geraldine a series of tests and have found she's well above her year in most areas. Whatever the previous fourteen governesses might have lacked, they were clearly decent tutors. She's very bright and quite advanced."

"I'm delighted to hear it." He did not sound delighted.

"I believe she will make you proud," Eleanor said, and realized almost instantly that it was the wrong thing to say. Of course it was the wrong thing to say. The child was not his. Geraldine was his ward, not his daughter. It was entirely possible that the only proud day of his life would be the day she reached her majority and was no longer his responsibility.

And none of that was her business, as Mrs. Redding had suggested.

"I'm sorry," she said quickly, before he could respond. Then, as if the apology needed explanation, she pushed on. "I always wanted to be a teacher when I was younger, but then I took a little bit of a detour."

"Into a number of office positions in London," he said, without consulting any notes. Meaning he just knew that. Eleanor told herself that wasn't strange at all, and there was absolutely no reason that prickling feeling should intensify until she felt goose bumps on her arms.

"Yes," she confirmed. "This governess position is new to me. Perhaps in my enthusiasm, I've overstepped."

For a long moment, Hugo said nothing. But it wasn't as if his silences were empty. On the contrary, everything felt thick. The air. That raw thing that kept expanding inside her chest, until once again, she didn't think she could pull in a full breath. But the longer she stared at his mesmerizing face, and those unholy eyes of his, the less she cared.

"You do not treat me like a monster, Miss Andrews." Hugo's voice was a smooth lick against the quiet that surrounded them. "I find it disconcerting that you do not, when everyone else does. Why don't you?"

Eleanor felt her lips part at that, and quickly snapped her mouth shut. "I don't know what you mean."

"I think you do. Women normally approach me in one of two ways. They either fling themselves at me, desperate for my touch and my attention. Or they cower, certain that a stray graze of my finger will ruin their reputations forever, and more importantly, leave them mere, shivering wrecks of their former selves thanks to my supposed evil powers—but not in any fun way. Yet you do neither."

There was a note in his voice that she didn't understand, but it seemed to wind its way through her like honey. Or something far more intoxicating.

"I apologize, Your Grace," she managed to say. "I was unaware that a certain reaction was called for the part of the job. To you, I mean. Perhaps it's silly of me, but I thought my relationship with Geraldine was the point."

"No one takes this job for the child. One way or another, they always take it for me. The fact that you do not wish to admit this only makes you more curious. And I should not have to tell you that making yourself the focus of my attention…has consequences."

Eleanor was clenching her hands together entirely too tightly, something she only noticed when they went numb. She forced herself to unlace her fingers and sensation came back in a rush. She ignored it when they began to sting.

"I would prefer not to be crass, Your Grace, but you give me no choice."

"I am all ears, of course. I enjoy crassness very much. You must realize this."

"I'm sure you're a very nice man. Deep down," she added at his snort. "But of course you must realize that the position's salary is what's attractive. While you have a certain charm, I suppose, that really isn't why I came. I told you before. I was assured—repeatedly—that I would never see you."

"I have a very large and extraordinarily healthy ego, Miss Andrews, and yet it withers before you. Most women would scramble up the Cliffs of Dover if they imagined they might catch a glimpse of me."

"I suspect your ego is quite robust and will survive handily. And I am not most women."

"You most certainly are not."

Eleanor caught herself before she flung something back at him. There was no call to come over all caustic and acerbic, which seemed to be her happy place where the Duke was concerned. It wouldn't help her in any way to actively antagonize him. Hugo might have been eyeing her in very much the same way a large, indolent house cat might an extremely foolish mouse. But that didn't mean she should scamper out there of her own volition and show him her belly.

Think of the money, she told herself sternly. *Think of Vivi.*

She surged up and onto her feet at that. "It's late, Your Grace."

"It is not yet midnight." He didn't bother to glance at the watch on his wrist, which Eleanor could tell must have cost a fortune or two, since it looked like it belonged on the side of an old town hall in Prague. "It is scarcely ten."

"Which is late for those of us who rise with small children in the morning."

"There it is," he said softly and, if she was not mistaken, with some satisfaction. "There is that fear of me I recognize."

"It's not fear, it's anxiety," she corrected him. "It makes me anxious to have these confusing conversations. Surely you can understand that. I work for you."

"Of course I can't understand any such thing. I've never worked for anyone in all my days."

Eleanor waved a hand at the stuffed shelves on all sides. "Thank goodness you have all these books, then, to allow you a different perspective than your own."

"I think you're lying again, Miss Andrews," Hugo said, and his voice had gone silky. Dark. Something much worse than simply decadent.

And it shuddered through Eleanor. It made her ache. Everywhere.

Her pulse fluttered about weakly and she thought perhaps she shouldn't have had those prawns for her tea. Then she wondered what had become of her that she was standing here, actively wishing she was ill. Instead of the alternative.

"You've lost me once again," she told him. Faintly.

"What you're feeling right now is not fear," Hugo told her, and there was that certainty again. Pouring out of him as if he'd never suffered a moment's doubt about anything in his charmed life. "Or anxiety about speaking to your employer. You can feel how quickly your heart beats, can you not? And that hot and restless yearning in the pit of your stomach?"

She flushed hot and, she feared, red. "No."

"The funny thing about a man like me is that I cannot abide lies to my face. There are too many in print." He smiled. "Try again."

"I'm a bit overtired, actually. I'd like to be excused so I can take to my bed, please."

"Bed is the cure, Miss Andrews, but I'm not talking about sleeping. And I think you know it."

Eleanor found she was gaping at him. Again. And this time, she didn't have it in her to do anything about it.

"Are you… You can't…"

And Hugo laughed, stealing the heat from the fire and the air from the room.

Then, worse, he unfolded himself from his chair and rose to his feet. And suddenly, the library seemed like a closed fist—a vicious and unbreakable grip all around her. Forget breathing—Eleanor wasn't sure she could stand. But she also couldn't seem to move away the way everything in her screamed she should. It was as if she was frozen in place, though there wasn't a single part of her that was cold.

Not one.

"You look very much like a woman who can think of nothing at all but the way I might kiss you," Hugo said softly.

"That can't happen," Eleanor breathed.

"It already has. It will again. I'm afraid it is inevitable."

He reached over and fit his hands to her cheeks. And as if that was not bad enough, he used one thumb to trace slowly, lazily over her mouth, as if he was learning the contours of her lips.

If he'd doused her in gasoline and lit a match, she could not have burned hotter. Or brighter. And god help her, it was all so *wrong*.

"See?" His voice was so low, so sure, it seemed to interfere with her ribs. "Not fear at all."

He shifted, lifting her chin and her face toward his, and Eleanor panicked. Or anyway, that was what she thought that was, that blinding rush of sensation that was too electric and too impossible to be borne.

"I'm asexual," she blurted out.

She expected that announcement to stop him. To stop everything. To make all of this stop pulsing and whirling and make a little sense again.

But Hugo made a noise, deep in his throat, that sounded like a cross between a laugh and a sort of growl. He didn't let her go. If anything, his hands held her faster. And she felt them in even more places.

"Are you?" He didn't sound particularly fussed.

"Well, yes." This close, it was almost impossible to remember what she meant to say—it was those eyes of his. And worse, his mouth. His lush, wicked mouth, that hovered far too close to hers and made everything in her a molten sort of heat. "I always have been, I suppose."

"Have you?"

"Yes," she said, with a bit more asperity. She would have kicked herself if she could. And if she could remember how to operate her legs. "I don't feel things, you see. I'm sorry if that makes things awkward."

"It would," Hugo agreed. He moved closer to her, making his impossibly well-formed chest part of the whole…problem. "But I think you feel quite a lot."

"I most certainly do not," Eleanor retorted, despite the fact that she did indeed feel entirely too much. Everywhere. And constantly. And she couldn't tell if she was sick or panicked or something in between. But she was certain there was some other explanation than the heat she could see in his whiskey-colored eyes.

"I suspect that what you've been, little one," Hugo murmured, his voice a low rumble that she could feel inside of her like a kind of earthquake, "is bored."

And then he set his mouth to hers, and proved it.

CHAPTER SEVEN

THIS KISS WAS different from the last.

Eleanor would not have imagined in a million years that she would ever be in a position where she was noting the difference between kisses, having never expected to spend much time kissing anyone, but here she was. This one was different than the lazy way he'd taken her mouth in the hall outside the nursery.

Much different. Much…hotter.

There was urgency this time. Bright fire and driving need.

Or maybe, she thought with no little wonder, that was her.

Hugo dropped his hands from her face and slid them down her back. He pulled her up against him, and it was as if everything inside her head simply went white. Blank. She disappeared into the sound of her heart, clattering wildly against her ribs, and the impossible, wild beauty of his mouth on hers.

Over and over again.

In some distant part of her mind, Eleanor knew

this was a mistake. *She knew it*. But she couldn't seem to stop herself. She didn't *want* to stop herself. He angled his head and took the kiss deeper. Hotter. Wetter and wilder.

And she was content to let him guide her. Teach her. Take her over and burn her alive.

He kissed her again and again, bending her backward as he did. One of his hands found the small of her back and held her fast against him as he continued to use that mouth of his like some kind of slick weapon. Eleanor found her arms around his neck, but had no memory of putting them there. Maybe there was something inside of her that knew she needed to hold on. Or be lost forever in this storm she should have had the good sense to avoid.

But she didn't want to avoid it. She wanted to dance in it. She wanted to shout down the thunder and let the rain wash her clean.

She didn't even know what that meant, but she wanted it, and every time he dragged his lips across hers, she thrilled to it.

And then there was what he did with his hands. She couldn't work out which was worse, that he seemed to know her so much better than she knew herself, or that she was afraid she might explode with every sizzling new touch.

He slid his free hand down her side as if he was testing her shape, spilling heat wherever he went, then sliding around to grip her bottom and pull her even closer.

"Perfect," he muttered against her mouth, and

a sheer, shivery sort of reaction burst inside of her at that.

Pleasure, she thought. *Pure pleasure.*

She had never allowed herself that sort of thing before. She hadn't known it existed, if she was honest. But Hugo's hands on her body opened up a new window into near-unimaginable delights and Eleanor couldn't seem to keep herself from tossing herself headfirst into them. Whatever they were. Whatever the price.

"More," Hugo said in a low, dangerously gruff voice, moving his mouth down the line of her neck.

And when the world seemed to shift, the floor moving beneath them and the fire spinning in a giddy loop, it took Eleanor a moment to realize that it was because Hugo was doing it. She didn't think her feet hit the ground as he picked her up and swung her around until her back was to the bookshelf.

Then he pressed himself against her as if he couldn't bear another inch of separation between them.

Eleanor supposed she should have objected to that—to all of it—but she was entirely too busy being overwhelmed by him. All of him. Her mind could hardly keep up with what was happening to her body. What he was *doing* to her body.

And what her body was doing to her, every time she shivered. Every time she surrendered. Every time she let out sounds she didn't recognize.

Hugo's mouth was a torment. A reward. Both at once.

He stroked his hands down the length of her arms and threaded his fingers with hers. Then, never breaking contact with her lips, he lifted her arms up above her and pinned her wrists to the bookshelves at her back.

"Stay still," he ordered her.

And it didn't occur to Eleanor to do anything but obey him. She was quivering too much. She was too undone. She was lost in this, whatever it was, and she wasn't sure she could make her way out of it.

Scarier still, she wasn't sure she wanted out in the first place.

Hugo muttered something that she couldn't quite make sense of, and then he shifted back slightly so he could look down at her, moving his hands so that one rested on each side of her face. In some far-off corner of her mind it occurred to Eleanor to worry that he might find her lacking. That looking at her the way he was might break this spell, whatever it was. Because this was a man who could sleep with any of the great beauties of their age at will. And had.

But when he finally dragged his gaze back to hers, all thoughts and insecurities vanished. Because Eleanor might not have done this before. She might have no idea how this had happened or what she was meant to do next. But she'd never seen anything so hot or so needy in all her life as that look on Hugo's face.

It was so intense it felt like a kind of devastation, rolling over her and flattening her and changing her, but she was still standing.

Somehow, she was still standing, and she couldn't seem to step away from him. She couldn't even bring herself to try.

Hugo moved then. He traced his way down her neck, then moved his hands to cup her breasts, making her breath desert her in an audible rush that embarrassed her, it was obvious. But there was something reverent in the way his hands curved around her, testing her through the layers she wore and dragging those expert thumbs of his over her nipples— and the crazy part was that she could still feel the heat of his palms. Flooding into her. Making her feel even more needy and wild.

He made another one of those distinctly male noises deep in his throat, low and somehow untamed, that made everything inside Eleanor bristle into a kind of liquid awareness. Shocking and bright, even as it pooled low in her belly.

"Later," he said, and it sounded like a promise.

Eleanor had no idea what he was talking about. And she didn't care, because he kept going. He bent closer to her as he traced his way down the length of her body, finding the indentation of her waist and then the swell of her hips and taking his time learning both.

And then he found his way to the fastening of her trousers, and it was as if everything inside of her toppled over and crumbled into dust. Just like that.

"I told you not to move your hands." Hugo's voice was dark, demanding.

And it wasn't until he spoke that Eleanor realized

she'd brought her hands down toward his shoulders. To push him away? To draw him closer? She had no idea. But she did as he asked, because she couldn't think of what else to do, and she raised her arms back up over her head again.

And Hugo simply pulled the fastening of her trousers open, then dipped his hand inside, as if it was inevitable.

It felt as if it was.

There was no sound in the library. There was the snap and rustle of the fire, and then a harsh sort of noise that it took Eleanor long moments to realize was her own breathing. Panting, more like, that she could barely hear over the noise in her head that she thought was her heart. Beating madly.

But if Hugo heard any of it, he liked it. That was what that hard smile on his beautiful face told her. She could feel it wash over her like its own sort of glare, making her feel exposed. As if he could see things she wasn't even aware she was showing.

"I'm pleased that you're allowing this experiment, little one," he said, a certain satisfaction in his voice that should have alarmed her. She knew it should have, but she couldn't quite bring herself to react to it. "Given how well you know your own desires."

"I don't know what you…"

"Hush."

Once again, Eleanor obeyed him. Because he was sliding his fingers down, down, all the way into her panties, and that made everything in her…constrict. Shudder.

And then he curved his fingers around to cup her where no one else had ever touched her.

Eleanor realized as her legs went to jelly that she lacked the ability to stand.

But Hugo was holding her up with that big body of his and one hard hand at her hip. Even when he let out the sort of laugh that should have been outlawed as a public safety hazard, he kept her upright.

"I must tell you, Miss Andrews, you are remarkably wet for one who claims she is asexual."

"Wet?" she asked. On a choppy little breath.

"Very, very wet," Hugo amended, his voice little more than a dark growl.

And then he began to stroke her.

Sensation buffeted her from all sides. He was all around her. He loomed above her, and his shoulders blocked out the rest of the house, and more, the world she could hardly recall outside it. She could smell him, an intriguing male scent that put her in mind of the fire behind them and soft, buttery leather, only much warmer. She could taste him in her mouth, like the kind of spirits she only dared sip at Christmastime, and then only in minuscule quantities.

And she could feel him. Good god, could she feel him.

He moved the hand at her hip back to her jaw, smoothing his palm around to hold her where he wanted her. And there was a smile on his face when he lowered his head to take her mouth once more.

Eleanor could taste that, too. And god help her,

he was like a bottle of the good stuff, with every demanding slide of his tongue against hers.

And all the while, he stroked her. He slipped in and around her folds, slippery and hot when she'd never felt anything like it before. When surely it should mean something was wrong, but nothing *felt* wrong.

Eleanor couldn't think. She couldn't control herself. She was lost between his mouth and his hand, and she simply followed the rhythm he set as he built that storm in her.

Higher and higher. Darker and wilder.

And she didn't know when it dawned on her that it was going to break. That the tightness in her belly and the need and the hunger could only go one way, and it was going to happen whether she wanted it or not. That the wall that seemed to bear down on her was entirely unavoidable, and coming much too fast—

"Don't fight it, little one," Hugo murmured. He lifted his mouth from hers the slightest little bit, so Eleanor could taste his words on her lips.

"I'm not fighting anything," Eleanor gasped out. Crossly.

But then it was happening.

It was like a golden sort of crash, fast and slow at once. A shower of fire and sparks, magic and longing, as debilitating as it was delicious. It roared through her, from the top of her head straight down to the tips of her toes that she dug into the floor beneath her feet as if that could keep her holding on.

She bumped against his marvelous, wicked hand and she threw her head back, and still his mouth was there against her neck, urging her on. Taking her wherever he wanted to take her, and all she could do was let him.

He was even laughing slightly, she noticed with something like panic, as she fell and fell and fell.

And hoped like hell that Hugo would catch her on the other side.

Making his starchy little governess come apart beneath his hands was the hottest thing Hugo could remember doing.

Ever.

The little sounds she made. The dazed wonder in her wide eyes. Even that frown at the end, and her sharp little voice before she broke to pieces.

He didn't understand how it was possible when he should have no further to sink, but Eleanor Andrews was ruining him.

But Hugo shoved that aside. For any number of reasons, not least of which was the fact that he had already been ruined. A long, long time ago. There was no lower place for Hugo Grovesmoor to go. He should know. He'd tried to find it over and over again.

And no innocent woman deserved a man that self-destructive. Especially not a woman like this one, who had confused her own inexperience for disinterest. That was how little she knew of men.

He would eat her alive.

And it said something about him, didn't it, that he rather liked that idea.

She was limp and dazed and breathing heavily, so he shifted her off the bookcase and swept her up into his arms, entirely too aware of the way she melted against him. He carried her over to the wide sofa and settled her on it, more than a little concerned about how uncharacteristically gentle he was with this woman. Automatically. When he was not exactly known for his sweet bedside manner. He did not lounge around, shyly reading verses of poetry from slim volumes and softly asking permission to touch a lover's ankle.

Please.

Hugo had always assumed that what poetry was in him was rough and raw and best expressed with his hands. And his body.

And the dark things he could do with both. And did, again and again.

He'd never had any complaints. In person, that was. The tabloids were a different story, but even those fabricated fantasies never claimed he was a bad lover. Simply that he was a very, very bad man.

But still. Untried innocence was not his thing. No matter how sweet the taste, still there on his tongue. Driving him that much closer to madness.

He made himself stand, something furious in his chest and all that leftover heat and hardness making his trousers feel too tight, and waited for her to come back to him.

It took her a long time. And it occurred to him

that a woman who fancied herself asexual and was so obviously a stranger to her own body was perhaps significantly less experienced than he'd been thinking. Almost as if she was something more than "inexperienced." Almost as if…

But that was impossible, of course. This wasn't the dark ages.

"Are you a virgin?" he asked, perhaps a bit too abruptly.

On the deep leather couch, Eleanor stirred. She looked around as if she didn't know where she was, and didn't recognize the library either way. Or him. She sat a little bit straighter as she took him in. Her hands went first to her head and she smoothed back the one or two strands that had dared to come loose from that ruthless bun she always wore. Only then, when she'd secured her dark hair in its cage, did she shift against the seat, look down, and note that her trousers were still wide open.

And Hugo found he was captivated by the red flush that took her over, staining her cheeks and making her brown eyes gleam from beneath her fringe with that hint of honey that he thought might be his undoing.

Eleanor swallowed, hard, and he saw a frown etch itself between her eyes again. But she didn't say anything. She only fastened her trousers and sat a bit straighter. Only then did she look up at him, and something about the steady way she did it made him feel like the monster he knew he was. More so than usual, that was.

She looked breakable.

It should have made him hate himself all the more, that he should so effortlessly stain whatever he touched. But that was not his primary reaction to the mounting evidence that no one had touched Eleanor but him.

Indeed, what he was feeling—in every part of him, like a thread of wild heat—was significantly more primitive.

"Whether I am or am not a virgin, I can't imagine how that's any of your business at all," she said coolly. Her brows rose slightly. Arrogantly, he would have said, had anyone ever managed to outdo him in that arena. "Your Grace."

And Hugo stopped feeling badly about the whole thing.

"That is not a very nice tone to take with a man who just made you come," he pointed out, all silk and threat. "So hard you nearly broke off the shelf of an ancient bookcase."

"The bookcase appears to be holding up just fine."

"Given that you had your back arched and your eyes closed while you rode my hand, I rather doubt you have the slightest idea how close you came to bringing down the whole of my collection on your head."

"I wish it had," she said, and while her gaze grew darker, her tone only chilled further. "Everything that's happened here is almost too inappropriate to bear. I will tender my resignation in the morning, of course."

Hugo lifted one shoulder, then dropped it. "If you wish. But it will be a wasted effort. I won't accept it."

She scowled at him. "Of course you will."

He didn't know why she amused him. She shouldn't have. He'd fired many of her predecessors for far less than this. The one who'd tracked him down in the gardens to let him know she was without her undergarments. The one who'd pouted prettily at him over Geraldine's head when the child had needed a doctor. The alarming one who'd left lavender-scented unmentionables all over the house, for servants and Hugo alike to find in the most curious of places. He hadn't thought twice about sacking any of them.

He should have welcomed Eleanor's resignation. Hell, he should have demanded it himself the moment he'd seen her outside the nursery, divested of that awful coat and obviously a problem. With killer curves.

Hugo had no idea what the hell was wrong with him.

"I fear I must remind you—and not for the first time—that I am the Duke of Grovesmoor."

"I know who you are. Everybody knows who you are."

"Then you should know how pointless it is to argue with me." He watched as she rose to her feet, and didn't bother to hide his satisfaction when she had to reach out a hand to steady herself. "Instead of discussing resignations that will never come to pass, why don't you tell me why you insist on scraping your hair back into that painful-looking bun?"

"Because it's professional," she snapped. "And also none of your business."

Hugo kept his gaze trained on hers. Very slowly, very deliberately, he lifted his hand and put the fingers he'd sunk deep inside of her softness into his own mouth. Then licked them clean.

Her mouth fell open. Her pretty face went pale, then red.

"I can still taste you, Eleanor," he said, a bit more roughly than planned, because she affected him too damned much. "It's a bit too late for boundaries, don't you think?"

Eleanor flinched. And he wasn't at all surprised when she turned around, then fled the library and his presence, coming as close to running from the room as a person could without actually breaking into a sprint.

Hugo didn't blame her at all.

He blamed himself. And the fact he really could taste her, sweet and sharp and intoxicating, was his own cross to bear as the night wore on. As he sat in his library and brooded into his fire and contemplated just how destroyed he was. How much of a monster was he, really, if he'd become the disreputable, distasteful Old Duke locked away in his ancient house, terrifying virgins? Why not simply start belching out flames and singeing the livestock, while he was at it?

But when the next day came and went with no resignation letter on his desk and Eleanor still in

residence, his commitment to his self-flagellation…
shifted.

Because it was one thing to lure an unwilling virgin into his dragon's lair.

It was something else again when she knew who he was, and what he might do…and stayed anyway.

CHAPTER EIGHT

"You have a visitor."

Eleanor looked up from the textbook she and Geraldine were poring over in the grand library to see Mrs. Redding standing over them, looking more crisp and disapproving than usual. Which was quite a feat.

"A visitor?" she echoed, trying to work out from the other woman's expression what that could possibly mean. Eleanor didn't know anyone in the area. Aside from a few rambles about the village with Geraldine, she hadn't spent much time off Hugo's estate in the five and a half weeks she'd been here.

"It is not encouraged for staff to invite friends and family to the estate," the housekeeper said coldly, as if she'd caught Eleanor throwing a party like an errant teen. "We are not guests of His Grace. We are members of his staff. I'm certain this was covered extensively in the interview with the placement agency."

"I haven't invited anyone," Eleanor protested, but it was no use. Having rendered her judgment, Mrs.

Redding had already turned and was making her brisk way to the door, every line of her body showing her offense at Eleanor's transgression.

Eleanor gave Geraldine a reading assignment to keep her occupied, then followed Mrs. Redding's crisp footsteps toward the front of the house.

There was only one person who knew where she was, but there was no way Vivi would be here, surely. Vivi preferred to stay in the bright lights of London, or in the posh homes of friends abroad. She certainly didn't venture into the north of England. Under any circumstances.

That's a bit harsh, isn't it? she chastised herself as she walked.

Something was the matter with her. It had been growing inside of her since that terrible night in the Duke's private library a week ago. As if he'd infected her with his touch. With the things he'd made her feel. She found herself tense and strange. Snappish with Vivi on the phone and even less able to sleep than she had been before.

It was her horror with her own behavior, she told herself stoutly as she made her way toward the great foyer. She'd allowed herself to be compromised and worse, she kept letting it happen.

The Duke hadn't touched her again, which meant it was all she thought about.

But what he was doing was worse. Dropping by Geraldine's lessons as the mood took him, for example, when Eleanor had assumed he was off somewhere else being Hugo on his usual international stage.

"This does not sound like the Latin I was forced to learn," Hugo had said from behind her, out in the back gardens one unexpectedly fine morning, making Eleanor jump as she walked and then instantly try to conceal her reaction from Geraldine.

"It's French," Eleanor had said sternly.

"I am aware of that, thank you," Hugo had replied as he'd moved to walk beside her. In French, which had made Geraldine giggle.

And Eleanor had wanted nothing more than to ask him to leave them to their walk and French conversation, but, of course, she couldn't. It was his property. And his ward, for that matter. But she'd been psyching herself up to demand he respect Geraldine's lesson time when he started talking to the little girl directly.

In perfect French, unlike Eleanor's, which had been cobbled together from her time in school and the job she'd had for a year when she was barely twenty at a French company based in England.

And he kept it up for the better part of the next twenty minutes, as if Eleanor wasn't there.

It had made her heart beat a little too fast in her chest. And it had made Geraldine glow, which was worse—because Eleanor had no defense against her scrappy charge.

And when he took his leave he bowed to Geraldine and only pinned Eleanor briefly with an unreadable look in his dark whiskey eyes. That had haunted her long after.

"Come have dinner with me," he'd said another afternoon, appearing in the library when Eleanor had thought she and Geraldine were on their own.

Eleanor had instantly checked to see where the little girl was, but she was still at one of the tables in the center of the huge library, poring over a dictionary as she picked ten vocabulary words to use in the new story she was writing in the journal Eleanor had her keep.

"I appreciate the offer, Your Grace," she'd said as frostily as possible. *"But I'm afraid that's impossible."*

"For all you know I intended to whisk you off to Rome for the evening."

Eleanor scowled at the book in front of her, though she'd stopped seeing the words on the page in front of her the moment he'd materialized at her side. *"That would be almost incomprehensibly inappropriate."*

"I would hate to be incomprehensible," Hugo had murmured in that sardonic tone of his that made her think of his body pressed against hers and his clever hands between her legs. *"My private dining room will have to do."*

"That is equally inappropriate," she'd said sharply.

"But more comprehensible."

"Your Grace—"

"It's a bit late for that, Eleanor," he'd said quietly. *"Don't you think?"*

"I do not think," she'd retorted, struggling to keep

her voice in a whisper. She'd glanced at Geraldine, then back at Hugo again. *"This is a game to you. But it's a job to me. And more people than just me depend on it."*

Hugo's impossible mouth had shifted into one of those half smiles that haunted Eleanor when she slept. And when she wasn't sleeping, too.

"If I hadn't tasted your innocence myself I'd assume that meant you had a child of your own hidden away somewhere."

"I don't have a child, I have a sister," Eleanor had said in an undertone.

"A younger sister?"

"Vivi is twenty-five."

"And she is unwell?"

Eleanor had frowned at him. *"No, she isn't unwell. But I'm the one who pays the bills."*

One of Hugo's brows rose. *"You pay for your twenty-five-year-old sister?"*

And it had occurred to Eleanor that she'd never had to explain her situation to anyone before. Most people didn't ask such impertinent questions and if they had, she wouldn't have felt compelled to answer them.

"It's complicated," she'd said after a moment. *"Vivi is very talented, but it's not always easy to find the right place for her to shine. Once she does, everything will seem a good deal more...balanced."*

There had been something entirely too perceptive in Hugo's gaze, then.

"Are you trying to convince me?" he'd asked. *"Or yourself?"*

When Geraldine had called out that she was finished, breaking the tight little knot that had seemed to hold them both where they stood, Eleanor had been unreasonably grateful.

Hugo made her feel like she no longer fit in her own body.

Not that she felt much like herself now, she was forced to admit as she hurried along the main floor toward the foyer.

Who exactly are you? a little voice asked from deep inside her, and to her shame it sounded a little too much like Hugo's. *Who exactly are you so desperate to hold on to?*

She shook her head to get that voice to shut up, for a change. And then she turned the final corner that delivered her into the great foyer and stopped.

Because Vivi was standing there.

For a moment, Eleanor couldn't make any sense of it.

There was no reason on earth for Vivi to be in Yorkshire, much less in the grand foyer of Groves House. Back in London, when Eleanor had asked if her sister planned to come up and visit her when she finally got a break after her first six weeks, Vivi had been noncommittal.

I can't possibly know what I'll be doing so far in the future, she'd said. Dismissively, Eleanor thought now. But at the time she hadn't thought much of it. That was Vivi's style, after all. So effervescent and carefree that she never knew what she was going to be doing from one moment to the next, much less six weeks out. *But I doubt very much that I'll have any business in Yorkshire.*

But she'd said *Yorkshire* the way some people might say *nuclear waste facility.*

Eleanor told herself she had to be mistaken, but the woman who stood at the other end of the foyer was indisputably Vivi. She was microscopically thin, the better to show off the excruciatingly expensive designer jeans she wore thrust down low on her jutting hipbones. The denim licked down her minuscule thighs before disappearing into a pair of recognizably chic boots. She wore the sort of coat and scarf that would not look out of place in Sloane Square, and she wore her hair in the usual temperamental way. It was wild and wavy, pouring down her back and over her shoulders in an artful sort of tangle that was meant to look as if it never saw a brush or a styling tool, when the fact was, it took hours for Vivi to make it look just so. As she moved closer, Eleanor could see that her sister's lips were pursed slightly as she took in the wealth on display across every inch of the deliberately jaw-dropping entryway. More, she had a particular gleam in her eyes that Eleanor recognized all too well.

Avaricious, that voice inside her whispered.

Eleanor told herself to stop. She was being severe and unfair. She should have been delighted to see her little sister. She was. Of course she was.

"Vivi? What are you doing here? Is everything all right?"

Vivi took her time meeting Eleanor's gaze. Her own lingered on the walls, on all that gold and gilt, stretching out in all directions. Statues and flowers and paintings that went all the way up to heaven and back. And that was just the foyer.

"Aren't you the dark horse," Vivi murmured.

"You don't look as if anything terrible has happened," Eleanor continued, telling herself that there was no need to read into her sister's dark tone.

Vivi eyed her, her hands stuck into the back pockets of her jeans and her hips thrust out in what could only be called an aggressive posture. Eleanor ignored that, too.

"You told me this place was a tired old mausoleum. A crumbling pile of rocks, plunked down in the middle of a moor with heather growing all over it like a weed." Vivi sniffed and jutted her chin at all the lavish displays before her. "Apparently not."

"You were the one who called it a pile of rocks," Eleanor pointed out, still keeping her voice calm and even and something like soothing. "I just didn't argue."

"I had no idea you were so secretive, Eleanor. Is that a new personality trait?"

"Surely you didn't really think that the Duke of Grovesmoor lived in a crumbling pile of stones." Eleanor made herself smile. "Given that he owns the better part of England."

"It's quite intriguing that you've decided you need

to keep secrets from me now that you work in such a posh old house, isn't it?"

There was no denying the fact that there was more than little attitude in her sister's voice. But Eleanor ordered herself to remain calm, and not only because she never called her miracle of a sister out on anything, much less *tone*. But because she couldn't trust the things that were happening inside of her.

The truth was that she hadn't felt much like herself since Hugo had kissed her that first time. Maybe Vivi was right and Eleanor had gone squirrely and secretive. She'd never done anything like that before.

And when, exactly, were you permitted to have any kind of a life before? that voice inside demanded. *Or have you forgotten that your whole existence is catering to Vivi's life, not yours? She just doesn't like imagining that anything might have shifted.*

It was possible that Eleanor didn't really like it all that much, either.

"If I failed to tell you something it wasn't for any nefarious reason," she said, still keeping her voice even. "I thought you knew everything there was to know about this position. You're the one who recommended I interview for it in the first place."

Vivi shook her hair back from her face, though none had fallen forward. "I assumed he'd thrown the kid in some second-rate cottage somewhere rustic. Not *this*."

Eleanor did not rise to the defense of *the kid*. She did not dig into Vivi's assumptions about rustic cottages. And she did not ask herself why it was apparently perfectly all right for her to live somewhere not quite as nice as Groves House. Because Vivi didn't mean it. Vivi came across as thoughtless, but only because every thought that moved through her head came out of her mouth, not because she harbored any ill will. It was part of the larger-than-life charm that Eleanor had been grateful for every single moment since Vivi hadn't died in the car accident that had claimed their parents.

She reached out a hand to place it on her sister's arm and build a bridge, but Vivi pulled away.

"Vivi, whatever is the matter?" she asked.

And she wasn't surprised when her sister's expressive eyes filled with emotion. Not quite tears, but their glassy precursor. This felt like normal, suddenly. Like common ground again. Vivi had problems and Eleanor fixed them. That was the way the world turned.

"Everything." Vivi's voice was ever so slightly husky, as if from the force of her feelings. "The rent wasn't paid. The credit card is full. The flat is a *complete* tip. I can't find anything and what I can find is filthy and I don't know what to do about any of it."

"You didn't pay the rent? And you went over the maximum on the credit card?" Eleanor shook her head, feeling dazed. "But I left you the money—"

"And that's not the worst of it. Peter's asked Sabrina to marry him." Vivi stared at Eleanor as if she should have an explosive response to that bit of news. Eleanor only blinked and Vivi made a frustrated, impatient sort of noise. "*Lord* Peter, Eleanor. Hello.

Only the man who's been crucial to my happiness for as long as I can remember."

"As long as you can remember," Eleanor repeated dryly.

Vivi waved a hand. "This past month, anyway. We've been *quite* close."

"And by this past month," Eleanor said, trying her best not to panic at what Vivi must have done to their finances in so short a time, "do you mean the month that I've been here, in this house that you might have noticed is miles and miles away from anything, teaching lessons to a seven-year-old child?"

"The point is that everyone thought that I was in with a chance," Vivi complained. "But he chose *Sabrina*, of all people. The cow. She's no better than she has to be and who cares if her father has all that money? But everything's gone pear-shaped." Vivi held Eleanor's gaze for a moment, then shifted to look around the foyer again, almost as if she was calculating something as she did. "It was time to make myself scarce, that's all. I thought I'd hole up with you for a little while."

"Vivi," Eleanor said softly. "What did you do?"

Her sister shrugged, though it was more of a defensive gesture than anything else. "Some people need to learn how to have a bit of a laugh, that's all."

Eleanor suddenly became very aware of where they were standing. The foyer appeared empty, but Eleanor had been in Groves House too long now. She knew that the Duke's staff were everywhere. That every word was being watched, recorded, judged.

That whatever Vivi might have done, the whole house didn't need to know about it.

Though it was entirely possible that all of England would, if she'd got up to her usual tricks. And found her way into the tabloids again. Of course, Vivi would likely view that sort of exposure as a great success.

"Come on," Eleanor said, reaching out once more and this time, actually taking hold of her sister's arm. "This is not the place to talk about this. We'll go somewhere a bit more private."

Vivi certainly didn't evidence any sense of urgency as she sauntered along, letting Eleanor keep hold of her as they walked. Eleanor didn't know why it made her teeth clench, hard. This was nothing new. This was who Vivi was. She never thought things through. The rent, the credit card, whatever idiotic thing she'd done to Lord Whoever and his new fiancée. She expected the whole world to revolve all around her, and because of that, it usually did.

Or Eleanor's did, anyway. It always had.

But Groves House wasn't the place for Vivi, something deep and dark in Eleanor's gut insisted. She couldn't let her sister take—

Eleanor was ashamed of herself. There was nothing here that was hers. There was nothing anyone could take from her, especially not the sister she loved. The sister she would give anything to if she had the chance. The sister who had somehow survived that accident, and kept Eleanor for being all on her own.

That was what she was telling herself, fiercely and on repeat, when she turned the corner that led toward the nursery wing where her rooms were and nearly ran straight into Hugo.

And she knew who she was then, in an instant. She knew too much about the feelings she'd been telling herself were uncertain for so long now. Particularly after what happened in his library a week ago. Oh, the lies she'd told herself to explain it all away…

But there was nothing but truth here, pouring into the hallway like the diffident light of the afternoon outside.

Eleanor did not want Vivi to meet Hugo.

There was something inside of her, hunched and ugly, all claws and spite. And it was dragging all of its sharp edges around and around in the pit of Eleanor's stomach, because it wanted to avoid this. It would have done anything to avoid exactly this.

She did not want Hugo to behold her vibrant, charming sister who wrapped men like him around her fingers.

Or tries, anyway, that ugly little voice hissed.

But it was too late.

Because Vivi recognized Hugo instantly. Of course she did. Eleanor knew her sister, but even if she hadn't she'd have understood the change in her sister's body language. Suddenly everything was languid, easy. Suddenly Vivi's eyes seemed smoky, and the little giggle she let out was the same.

Eleanor had never wanted to slap her hand over

her sister's mouth before. Or at least, she'd never wanted it this badly.

"I had no idea, Miss Andrews," Hugo drawled, coming to a stop a few feet away, his dark gaze unreadable, "that governesses could multiply in the space of an afternoon. Like geese. How extraordinary."

Eleanor watched that gleaming gaze of his flick over her sister, and was more than a little surprised when it returned to her. But perhaps he was outraged. Perhaps he was looking for an explanation as to why he'd been kissing the likes of Eleanor when all the while he could have had Vivi.

And that ugly thing inside of her grew thicker. Burrowed deeper. But there was no stopping a speeding train, and Vivi had always been far more dangerous than any high-speed rail.

"Your Grace," Eleanor said stiffly, especially when Vivi seemed to melt into her side, holding on tight to Eleanor as if she was her very own plush toy. "May I present my sister, Vivi."

"You may," Hugo said in that same sardonic drawl that made heat bolt through Eleanor, but didn't seem to have the same effect on Vivi. "If you feel you must."

Eleanor frowned at that, but her attention was drawn by her sister, who couldn't seem to stop that damned giggle.

Be kind, Eleanor told herself sternly. Hugo was an overwhelming man. Anyone would be expected to overreact to the sight of him.

"I am honored, Your Grace," Vivi simpered. Then she batted her eyelashes at Hugo. "And here I thought every duke in the land was over the age of fifty."

"It only feels that way," Hugo replied with that liquid ease of his that made the bottom of Eleanor's stomach disappear. "It is the obsequiousness that ages a man, not the title."

Eleanor flushed on her sister's behalf, but it was a wasted effort as Vivi hardly seem to notice that the Duke had just taken her down a peg or two. Or perhaps she did notice. Perhaps that was her sister's true secret weapon, all this time. Maybe Vivi got her mileage out of pretending not to notice the very clear signals sent all around her.

But in either case, Eleanor frowned at Hugo, because she wasn't pretending anything.

"If you'll excuse us," she said, perhaps too severely, "I must show my sister to my rooms and then return to my duties."

"I'm sure Geraldine can manage," Hugo said offhandedly.

"Have you been supervising her reading, Your Grace? I had no idea you had taken such an active interest."

"I have been supervising my accounts," Hugo said in a faintly chiding tone that made Eleanor flush slightly. Again. "Which is how I know that I employ a veritable fleet of overpriced nannies. The child is more than fine. Always."

Vivi laughed again then, though there was nothing to laugh about in Eleanor's opinion. Then she let herself flop a bit toward Eleanor, as if she was giving her a hug from the side.

"You must forgive my sister, Your Grace," she said merrily. "She's ever so serious. She always has been. It won't surprise you to learn her favorite color is gray."

Eleanor told herself there was no reason for it, but that didn't stop the feeling of betrayal that swept over her. And the injustice of it, to have Vivi cut her down like that and call her *gray*, of all things, when it wasn't even true.

But there was nothing to be gained by arguing the point. There was no arguing with Vivi.

"My favorite color is not gray," Eleanor heard herself say, to her own astonishment. And once she'd started it seemed silly not to carry on. "On the contrary, I prefer a bright and cheerful red. It just so happens, however, that one cannot march about life forever dressed like a cardinal."

Next to her, Vivi slid Eleanor a cool look. She pretended not to see it.

But she was certain Hugo did. Just as she was certain that Vivi was about three seconds away from hurling herself across the space that separated them to make a complete fool of herself. All over him.

And the truth was, Eleanor could hardly blame her. She'd made a fool of herself over him herself, hadn't she? Such a fool of herself, in fact, that she hadn't even realized she was doing it until now.

When it was much too late.

Hugo was devastating. Full stop. Today he was

affecting his international rock star look again. His dark hair looked messy, the intriguing kind of messy that made Eleanor want to test it with her fingers. His dark eyes were lit with that suppressed humor of his, dark and sardonic. He wore another one of his battered T-shirts that left nothing of his perfect chest to the imagination and another pair of jeans that hugged him in all the wrong places, as if he aspired to give the two-fingered salute to the fusty dukedom with every breath and outfit. And as if there were no autumn drafts snaking along the halls and no wind rattling the windows, come to that.

Or as if he was immune to all of it, because he was that darkly beautiful.

But Eleanor was quite certain that all Vivi saw when she looked at him were pound notes.

"If you wish to wear red, I would not object," Hugo said, a current of dark laughter in his voice. "There is no required uniform, Miss Andrews. I hope Mrs. Redding didn't mislead you on that score."

"Oh, you silly old thing," Vivi cut in then, with a little trill in her voice, and though her eyes were on Hugo she was clearly speaking to Eleanor. Or pretending to, anyway. "You know that red doesn't suit you."

Hugo's attention swung back to her sister, and Eleanor was glad, because she felt stricken straight through. Ashamed, if she was honest with herself at last.

Had she really imagined that she was anything to

a man like this but a diversion while he was bored? Even for a moment?

She knew the way of the world. There was a reason Vivi was the one who flitted about with people of Hugo's ilk, and it wasn't only because she was thinner and prettier. It was because she bloomed in such circumstances. She came alive. She stole all the light from the room.

Men like Hugo were destined for women like Vivi. Women like Eleanor were destined to be exactly what she was here in Groves House: staff. And that was all right, she told herself fiercely as she watched her sister show her dimples to Hugo. Some people were meant for the shadows and Eleanor had long since accepted that she was one of them. She didn't know what had happened to her over the past nearly six weeks, stuck away in this rambling old house with only a seven-year-old to talk to. She'd started believing in the sort of fairy tales she read to Geraldine. Or she'd been tempted to, anyway.

She'd even let Hugo touch her.

When she knew—when everyone knew—that he was a man who toyed with others. And so what if he'd claimed the tabloids had lied about him? That was what he would say.

She didn't understand how she'd allowed herself to feel so many impossible things inside and then lie to herself about it. Because if she'd been as unaffected by Hugo as she'd claimed she was—as she'd been so sure she was—nothing Vivi was saying or doing could possibly have bothered her.

And that was the trouble. It bothered her a lot.

"You must bring your sister to dinner, Miss Andrews," Hugo said, snapping Eleanor back to the issue at hand, and she tried to stop noticing that his eyes looked like overpriced whiskey. Especially when she couldn't read the expression in them, as he looked from Eleanor to Vivi and then back again. "In my private room. Tonight."

"I would love to, Your Grace," Vivi trilled—but Hugo was already walking away.

Eleanor pulled her arm away from Vivi's then, and hated herself for it.

"There's no need to respond," she said matter-of-factly. "He is the Duke and this is his house. That was not a request or an invitation, it was an order."

Eleanor set off again then, aware that her sister was following behind her. And that Vivi was laughing softly under her breath, which the tight, thickening thing inside of her knew could only bode ill. But she refused to look over her shoulder to see. She refused to give in to the dark things sloshing around in her gut.

She refused to be the person she'd apparently become.

Eleanor finally reached her rooms, and threw her door open, beckoning for Vivi to come inside.

And then had to ask herself why she was surprised that her sister entered the room very much the way she had, back when she'd arrived. Staring all around at the sheer luxury. Eleanor found herself standing there in the sitting room, rooted to the floor as Vivi gave herself a tour, feeling awkward and angry and deeply disappointed in herself.

"My, my, my. This just gets better and better."

Vivi's faintly accusing voice floating in from one of the other rooms struck Eleanor in the heart. Because the truth was, she felt guilty. Horribly guilty.

And she knew why.

Her sister would have been here like a shot if she'd had any idea the sort of opulence that was on display at every turn in Groves House. That alone would have encouraged her. But Hugo's presence? Her sister would have done anything to meet the Duke of Grovesmoor. And Eleanor still couldn't explain to herself, not reasonably anyway, why she hadn't let Vivi know from the start that Hugo was in residence.

"You fancy him."

Eleanor's head shot up at that. She found Vivi leaning in the door that led from the sitting room to the bathroom, a considering look on her pretty face.

"Don't be absurd," she said. "He's my employer."

Vivi shook her head, and there was a sharp light in her eyes that Eleanor couldn't say she cared for at all. "Why else would you have lied to me?"

"I've never lied to you, Vivi. And you still haven't told me why you're here. Not the real reason."

"I missed you."

Something pointed seem to lodge in Eleanor's side, because she wanted that to be true. And she also knew it wasn't.

"I don't think so," she said quietly. "You've had

scandals and overdrawn bank accounts before without getting on a train. What makes this different?"

"I don't want to talk about London. It's so boring. What's not boring is you holed up in this gorgeous house with Hugo Grovesmoor. Something you failed to mention to me, night after night after night. If that's not a lie, Eleanor, I don't believe I know what one is."

"You were certain I would never encounter him," Eleanor replied, and she was aware of the fact that she was trying much too hard to keep her voice even. Though she allowed the slightest hint of impatience, as if this was one of Vivi's flights of fancy that she was called upon to temper. Because it should have been. "And I saw no reason to tell you of his comings and goings, because I hardly know when or if I'll lay eyes on him."

"You met him before today."

"Yes, I met him. If you consider being presented to him like any other member of staff 'meeting' him." She made quote marks in the air with her index fingers, and shook her head at her sister. "I think when you meet men it's a little more momentous than when I do."

She expected Vivi to argue. But instead, her sister only smiled. Which did not make Eleanor easy in any way, because she knew Vivi. There was always a scheme. There was always the next plan. The smile was never acquiescence.

Or worse, that little voice chimed in, *she agrees.*

When had she become so awful about her own sister?

And anyway, Vivi was changing the subject. "Why have I been shuffling about London, forced to spend my nights in a grotty bedsit, when you've been living it up like the landed gentry?"

"These are the governess's quarters," Eleanor said. She made herself smile. "This is what passes for a grotty flat to a duke."

"You are in terrible, terrible trouble, big sister," Vivi said, but if there was a storm, it had passed.

Once again, Eleanor saw before her the sister she knew. With a mischievous look in her golden eyes and an infectious grin. She blinked, doubting herself. It was as if she'd made her sister into some kind of enemy the moment she'd dared walk into the house—which said nothing nice about Eleanor. It said a whole lot, however, about jealousy and envy and a whole host of other, vile things that Eleanor didn't want to admit were sloshing around inside of her.

Congratulations, she thought. *You're a terrible person.*

"I know you have to work," Vivi continued merrily. "I'll take you to task later. In the meantime, I think I'll help myself to that glorious bath."

Eleanor stood there for a long while after her sister disappeared. After she heard the water turn on in the bathroom, splashing into the huge tub. She stood there and she tried to collect herself. She tried to remember the person she'd been before she'd come to this far-off place, and more, before she'd let Hugo touch her. Change her.

Make her into that jealous, dark-minded creature who was selfish beyond measure.

She told herself that it was over. That whatever the spell was that had held her in its grip these last weeks, Vivi's appearance had broken it. It was time to wake up and remember what she was doing here.

She made the money. Vivi was the one who reeled in men like Hugo. And for good reason. She was the sort of girl who caused scandals that ended up in tabloid newspapers. She was *someone*.

Eleanor had never been anybody.

She forced herself to leave, then. She closed the door to her own rooms quietly behind her and headed into the hall. She had to find Geraldine and get back to her job, which was the only reason she was here. The fact of the matter was that Vivi should never have come here, but she had. And worse, she'd run straight into the Duke within moments of her arrival, when he could have thrown them both out.

But he hadn't done that. And Eleanor knew why.

And if something lodged in her heart, making it feel cracked straight through, she told herself it was nothing.

Nothing at all. Nothing new.

Nothing that mattered.

CHAPTER NINE

HUGO COULDN'T SLEEP.

As he was not a man unduly plagued with the demands of conscience, this was not an issue he generally struggled with. But it wasn't some newfound and unruly set of principles that kept him up tonight, roaming his own halls like his very own ghost story.

It was Eleanor.

Eleanor, who he'd come to depend upon over these last weeks. For her starchiness. Her prim disapproval. Every spicy, challenging word that fell from her notably disrespectful mouth—the very same mouth that Hugo had tasted and which haunted him more than he cared to admit to himself, even now.

He had the terrible suspicion she would haunt him forever, not that he allowed himself to think such things. Not when he refused to think about next week, much less the rest of his life. Or anything approaching *forever*.

But the Eleanor he rather thought he'd come to know had disappeared tonight.

She'd been noticeably absent when he'd run into

her and her sister in the hall outside the summer salons, en route to the nursery wing. Gone was the fiercely capable Eleanor who'd been giving him hell and in her place was a far more quiet and distant version, as if she'd been trying to disappear where she stood.

Hugo hated it.

He'd never met Vivi Andrews before. But he knew her at a glance, because he knew her type intimately. It took him all of two seconds on his laptop to find entirely too much about the actual Vivi Andrews, and the sorts of shenanigans she got herself into with high-profile members of the aristocracy. The more he read about her, in fact, the less he understood about Eleanor. How was she so forthright and dependable when Vivi was anything but?

The truth was, the younger Andrews sister—who Eleanor was supporting, if he'd understood that right, which made no sense while Vivi pranced about decked out in the sorts of labels the heiresses of his acquaintance wore because their fortunes were so vast that a six-thousand-pound T-shirt was a "little treat"—was the sort of creature Hugo usually slummed around with. Vivi had showed him her true colors in their first meeting, all batting eyelashes and come-hither smiles as if they'd been in a club instead of a hallway in his ancestral home. And she'd kept it up throughout dinner while Eleanor sat beside her, subdued. Vivi had distinguished herself by being endlessly pouty, unkind at the slightest provocation, and obviously convinced that she was a great, rare

beauty when the truth was, thousands of equally ambitious girls looked just like her. Her sister was the
rare beauty, but he had no doubt Vivi wouldn't see
it that way.

She looked nothing like Isobel, and yet the resemblance was impossible to miss. Hugo felt Vivi's attention the way he'd always felt anything that
reeked a bit too much of Isobel's sort—like an oily
sort of shame inside him, as if the fact a person like
her was so obviously interested in him made him
somehow like them.

Because, after all, it had. Given enough time, he'd
become exactly who Isobel had made him, hadn't he?

He hadn't cared much for that thought, either.

"It astonishes me that you are sisters," he'd said
during their excruciating dinner.

Eleanor appeared to have taken it upon herself to
embody the very soul of the starchiest possible governess, with Victorian overtones. Her hair was more
severe than he had ever seen it before, wrenched
back from her poor face as if she was trying to pull
it out, so that only her fringe offered any kind of relief. And he doubted it was a coincidence that she'd
chosen to wear black. All black, save for a hint of
gray in the shirt she wore beneath her cardigan, as
if she was in mourning.

Or as if she was reacting to her sister's earlier
claim that it was her favorite color. A poke at Vivi,
he wondered? Or a twisted sort of penance?

"Don't be silly, Your Grace," Vivi had simpered
at him. She'd been in a slinky sort of red dress Hugo

thought would have been more appropriate for a club in Central London than a country duke's dining room. But the point was likely to draw his attention to all the skin the tiny dress left bare. "Everyone swears we are practically twins."

He was apparently not supposed to realize that she was being cruel.

But before he could express his feelings on that—which, it turned out, were extensive and a bit overprotective—Eleanor had sighed. Mightily.

"No one has ever said that. Not one person, Vivi. Anywhere." She'd aimed one of her chillier smiles at Hugo. "My sister and I are quite aware of our differences, Your Grace. We choose to revel in them."

Vivi laughed then, long and loud. The way Hugo had then realized, belatedly, she would continue to do all night. Because she clearly imagined she was being lively and full of fun, or whatever it was women like her told themselves to justify their behavior. He should be better versed in it, he knew. He'd heard it all before.

Sometimes from his own mouth.

He'd settled himself in for an endurance event. But it had turned out that he was more than capable of blocking out the likes of Vivi Andrews. She'd brayed on about the guest suite she'd been given while she remained in Groves House and something about her feelings regarding the Amalfi Coast, and Hugo had watched Eleanor disappear. Right there in front of him. She'd simply…gone away.

It had made Hugo edgy. And something far darker and more dangerous than that.

And now he was wandering his own damned halls, scowling at the portraits of men who looked like him, wondering why the plight of a governess and her family were getting to him like this.

Well. He wasn't wondering. He knew.

Watching Vivi create an entire character she called Eleanor—stiff and humorless and faintly doltish and unattractive—while Eleanor sat right there and was not only none of those things, but offered no defense against the brush that was being used to paint her, was maddening. But it was also familiar.

It was what Isobel had done to him.

He was in the grand ballroom, glaring out at the rain that lashed at what was left of the garden this far into fall, when he heard a faint noise from behind him. Hugo turned, and for a moment he couldn't tell if he'd conjured up the sight before him or if she was real.

But god, how he wanted her to be real.

Eleanor moved across the floor, light on her bare feet. She wore some sort of soft wrapper that showed him the better part of her legs and made Hugo wonder what was beneath it. But the thing that made his chest hurt was that finally, her hair was down. It wasn't ruthlessly scraped back and forced to lie flat and obedient against her skull. It was glossy and dark and swirled around her shoulders, making her look softer. Sweeter. Even that razor-sharp fringe seemed blurred.

Mine, he thought instantly.

And he wanted her so badly that he assumed this was a dream.

Until she stopped walking, jerked a little bit, and stared directly at him as if she hadn't seen him until that very moment.

"Are you hiding in the shadows deliberately?" she asked him, and even her voice was different this long after midnight. Softer. Less like a challenge and more like a caress.

"My ballroom, my shadows," Hugo said, and he hardly recognized his own voice, come to that. He sounded tight. Greedy. As if the need that pounded in him was taking over the whole of him, and the truth was, he wasn't sure he had it in him to care. "By definition, I think, I cannot be hiding. You should expect to see me anywhere you go in these halls."

Eleanor didn't respond to that. Her lovely face seemed to tense, as if it was on the verge of crumpling, and he couldn't bear that. He couldn't stand the idea of it. He'd told her that tears were anathema to him. He'd told her he put distance between himself and the faintest hint of them.

And yet he found himself moving toward her, his gaze trained on her as if he expected her to be the one who turned and ran.

"Why are you looking at me like that?" she asked, her voice a small little rasp against the thick, soft air in the old ballroom. The chandeliers were dim high above and it made the room feel close. Somehow intimate.

"You should not allow your sister to treat you like that," he told her, his voice much darker than it should have been. Much more severe. But he couldn't seem to do anything about that when it was taking everything he had to keep his hands to himself.

But Eleanor only shrugged. "You don't know Vivi. She doesn't mean anything by the things she says. Some people don't think before they open their mouths."

"You are mistaken," Hugo said, stopping when he was only a foot or so away from her, and still managing not to touch her. He expected her to move away from him. To bolt. Or square off her shoulders and face him with that defiance of hers that he'd come to look forward to in ways he couldn't explain to himself. Not to his own satisfaction. And not tonight, when neither one of them should have been here in this room where no one ventured by day. "Poison drips from every word she hurls at you. And you believe it. Sooner or later, you believe all of it."

Eleanor shook her head, though her gaze was troubled. "Vivi's young. She'll grow out of it."

"She's what? A year or so younger than you?"

"You don't understand the sorts of people she knows. Viciousness is a sport. When she's not trying to imitate them, she's really quite sweet."

But Eleanor's voice sounded so tired then.

"I know exactly how this story goes," Hugo told her quietly. "I've heard all these excuses before. I used to believe them all myself."

"You don't have a sister. And you don't understand. I almost lost her when we lost our parents. Who cares about a few thoughtless words?"

But Hugo cared. And the undercurrent in Eleanor's voice suggested she might, too, whether she wanted to admit it or not.

"I had a best friend," Hugo said softly. "And despite the fact we knew each other in the cradle, I eventually lost Torquil to the same poison that made me a villain in the eyes of the world. That's the trouble with the sort of hatefulness your sister seems so comfortable with. It doesn't go away. It doesn't fade. It corrodes."

"Isobel," Eleanor whispered.

Hugo didn't like her name in Eleanor's mouth. As if that alone could poison the woman who stood before him against him. Just the mention of her.

"Isobel and I dated, if that is what it can be called, for two weeks." He couldn't keep the bitterness from his tone. The truth was, he didn't really try. Because what was there now besides that bitterness? What was left? Only the stories Isobel had told about him, his inability to refute any of them, and the long game of revenge he was playing against all those who'd chosen to believe it. "Two weeks, that is all. There was no on-and-off nonsense, stretching on for years. There was barely any affair to speak of. There were two entirely physical weeks when I was too young to know better, and then I cut it off."

Eleanor's gaze searched his. "I don't understand."

"Of course you don't understand. I assure you, I do not understand it myself. Isobel didn't like the fact that while she wanted our relationship to be something more than it was, I did not." He felt his mouth flatten. "And she didn't see why she should have to accept any reality that she didn't like. So she made her own."

"You can't mean…" Eleanor took a deep breath that made her hair move about on her shoulders. And Hugo couldn't keep himself from reaching out then. If he was honest, he didn't try too hard.

He reached over and ran his fingers through the fall of her hair, dark and enticing. It felt warm against his fingers, as if she was giving off heat like some kind of sun, and as soft as he'd imagined. And when he was finished running his fingers through it—at least for now—he didn't let go. He held on to a hank of her hair, as if he needed it. As if it was some kind of talisman.

Or she was.

"At first it was just sad." He didn't like talking about any of this. It only occurred to him then that he never had before. Because who could he have told? Everyone had already come to their own conclusions. "She would contrive to be somewhere I was and the next thing I knew there was a photograph in a tabloid, and breathless speculation about whether or not we were back on. At first I didn't even realize that she was the one calling the paparazzi herself. But as time went on, of course, the coverage took a distinctly darker turn."

He didn't know what he expected from Eleanor. An instant refusal, perhaps. After all, Isobel had

been a sunny ambassador of goodwill. Everyone
said so. She had been all that was light and good
and the only strange thing she ever done in her life,
according to the coverage of her that she'd manipu-
lated constantly, was try to date a monster like Hugo.
It wouldn't have surprised him if Eleanor had argued with him. If she'd tried to deny the story that
he was telling.

But she didn't say a word. Her solemn gaze was
fixed to his, and she seemed ready enough to hear
him out.

No one else had ever given him that courtesy.
Hugo felt something sharp, wedged there in the vicinity of his heart, but he had no name for it.

"As time went on Isobel became more and more
unhinged. She got together with Torquil, of course,
but that wasn't enough for her. Because the truth was,
she knew that wouldn't hurt me. If he wanted to be
with her that meant nothing to me either way, and
that was what she couldn't stand. It was right about
the time she convinced my friend, who'd known me
all his life, that I'd treated her abusively in private
that it occurred to me her only real goal was to hurt
me. However possible."

"If you didn't care for her at all," Eleanor said
softly, "and you weren't even involved with her in
the ways she claimed, how could she ever have hurt
you?" She seemed to think better of that as she said
it. "Your friend's betrayal must have hurt, of course."

Hugo shrugged. "Sometimes a woman comes
between friends. To be honest, I wasn't worried. I

thought that he'd come out of it with continued exposure to her."

"I can't pretend to know how it feels to have lies about myself splashed all over the paper," Eleanor began.

"It was my father."

It sat there so starkly. That ugly little truth that Hugo had never dared utter out loud before to anyone but Isobel, and only that once. And not only because there was no one else to hear it. But because naming it gave it power and he had never wanted to do that. He had never wanted to give Isobel the satisfaction—not even in death.

"I was all the old man had," Hugo managed to say, aware there was a kind of earthquake in him, tearing through him and reducing him to rubble. And yet he stood. "And I was a terrible disappointment to him."

"I'm sure you're mistaken," Eleanor breathed, that honey in her dark eyes gleaming with sympathy. "Maybe you only thought he felt that way."

"I know he felt that way, little one." Hugo's voice was soft. "He told me so."

And he stopped trying to fight that feeling inside of him then. That sharp thing in his chest only seemed to bleed out more at that stricken look on Eleanor's lovely face. As if she couldn't imagine such a thing, that an old man could think so little of his only son.

But Hugo knew he had.

"My father was prepared to put up with a certain amount of foolishness, because he was old-school and he'd had what he called his 'day in the sun.' He very much believed that boys were indeed boys." Hugo felt his mouth curve, though it was no smile. "But his expectation was that such conduct unbecoming in a Duke of Grovesmoor would end. If not during my university years, then shortly thereafter. Except I met Isobel two years after I left Cambridge, when I was still committed to every wild oat a man could sow. And that was when she started her campaign."

"Surely your father didn't believe the tabloids."

"Of course not. My father would never sully his eyes with such trash. The trouble wasn't the tabloids themselves. It was that everyone who did read the tabloids accepted everything they read in them as fact. And it wasn't only the scandal rags. There were cleverly disguised hit pieces in more reputable magazines that made me seem seedy and vaguely disgusting. And soon enough, that was how I was discussed. Not just in salacious news programs, but right here, in my father's own home. To his face."

"Who would do something like that?" Eleanor asked, and if he hadn't been looking right at her, with her eyes wide and filled with distress, he might have imagined she was faking. "And why would your father believe the kind of person who would slander his own son directly to him?"

It was an excellent question, and one Hugo wished he could ask the old man.

"Sometimes a rumor is far worse than a fact," he said instead. "Facts can be proven or disproven, most of the time. But rumor can live on forever. It commands a life of its own and dignified silence doesn't refute it. And sooner or later, whether you mean to or not, you find that you're living in it. Against your will."

"There was nothing you could do?" She shook her head as if to clear it. "No way you could tell the truth?"

"That's the thing about rumors like that, little one," Hugo murmured. "They're *more* believable than the truth. My father was a man of the world. He'd flirted with his own share of potential scandals in his day. It made no sense to him that a pretty girl like Isobel, who could have anyone, would waste her time pretending to have a relationship with the one man who didn't want her. And I think you'll find that it didn't make sense to anyone else, either."

"But surely you could prove it."

"How?" Hugo wasn't surprised when Eleanor didn't have an answer. "Where there's smoke, people always look for a fire. And the more that fire burns, the more everyone believes that you must have had a hand in setting it, or you'd put it out. But Isobel had no intention of ever letting it die down."

He thought of that endless blue afternoon in all that Santa Barbara sunshine. The way Isobel had smiled at him.

You'll always be mine, Hugo. Always. No matter where you go or what you do, no one will ever see you without thinking of me.

"I'm surprised you didn't date her just to keep her

quiet," Eleanor said then, scowling furiously—but not, for once, at him. "Just to make her stop."

Hugo let out a low noise. "I thought about it, of course. But I didn't want to be anywhere near her. And then, of course, came Geraldine."

"None of this is her fault," Eleanor said at once. Fiercely.

"Of course not," Hugo said shortly. "I don't bear the child any ill will."

"But—"

"But I don't mind if the world thinks I do," he finished for her. He shook his head. "Before there was Geraldine, there was Isobel and her pregnancy. And believe me, she used it like a hammer." He dropped that piece of Eleanor's hair then, because his hands were curling into fists and he thought he'd better keep them to himself. "She told my father the child was mine."

"She left you. She married your friend. How could it be yours?"

"She didn't leave me." Hugo realized he'd growled that out like a savage, and fought for calm. "We were never together. But she told my father that we had been. And then she told him that I refused to do my duty. That I told her to get rid of it. That I was, in short, every bit the callous and unfeeling character she'd painted me in the tabloids. And in those rumors."

"You must have insisted on a blood test to prove that you're not the father."

"I did," Hugo bit out. "But he died before I could

show him that proof. He had heart failure and never recovered, and doctors can use any terms they wish to explain what happened. But I think the shock killed him."

He'd forgotten that they were standing in the middle of the ballroom. Because all he could see was Eleanor, and that terrible look on her face. As if there was nothing in the world but the two of them and the way they stood so close together, as if what he was telling her here was far more important than a mere story. As if it was something infinitely more critical than the past he was still paying for.

It was, he understood. He was telling her the truth about the most hated man in England, and she believed him.

She believed him.

Eleanor moved then, tipping herself up on her toes and fitting her palms to his chest. One of them right there where his heart still hurt.

As if she knew.

"I'm so sorry, Hugo," she whispered, her voice intense and low. "I'm ashamed to say I believed the stories, too."

Hugo felt a kind of bitterness twist through him then, though there was a warmth in it this time, as if it was something a little more complicated. He reached up and covered the hand over his heart with his.

"Do you know," he said quietly, "that you are the only person I have ever met who's apologized? When you are the one who's done the least damage."

She bit her lip, and electricity pounded through him, reminding him of all the ways this woman got to him. All the ways she was clearly the death of him.

"I've spoken to you as if I knew you. As if the stories I read were the truth, when of course they couldn't be. The truth is never so black and white, is it? No heroes, no villains, just people."

"Perhaps. But there are also Isobels in this world. They prey on others because they can. It gives them pleasure. And Eleanor, your sister is one of them."

She tried to pull her hand away, but Hugo held her fast.

"You don't understand," she said, her voice fierce again.

"But I do." Hugo moved closer then, until there was only the scantest bit of air between the two of them. "Tonight you're barefoot, your hair is down, every inch of you is feminine and soft."

"I didn't expect to run into anyone in what I wear to bed."

He took his free hand and placed it over her lips. He smiled down into the crease between her eyes. He felt things he'd never thought were real, before tonight.

"Eleanor. Who told you feminine and soft is bad?"

"Not bad," Eleanor said against his finger, sending delicious little licks of heat spiraling through him. "But not me." Her frown intensified. "It's cruel of you to pretend that you can't see it, now that you've met Vivi. I'm not the pretty one. I never was."

"Your sister is pretty, yes," Hugo said, dismissively. "In a very particular way that would, I imagine, appeal to a very particular man. But you?" He shifted his hands, smoothing them over her cheeks and then down to curl into the nape of her neck. "Little one. How can you not realize that you are beautiful? Stunning? There is no comparison."

Her marvelous eyes filled with emotion. Her perfect mouth trembled.

"You don't have to lie to me, Your Grace," she whispered.

And Hugo didn't know what to do with a woman who'd believed that he was a better man than anyone had believed him to be in years—making everything inside him shift and change—but not that she was the most beautiful creature he thought he'd ever beheld.

So he did the only thing he could. He kissed her.

CHAPTER TEN

IT WAS LIKE DANCING.

Eleanor wasn't sure she should let herself fall into something that felt a little too much like a fairy tale here in the middle of a ballroom, but his mouth was on hers again and she couldn't seem to think of anything else. Or she didn't want to think about anything else.

She didn't want to think about how little she'd cared for her sister tonight, which made her feel small. Petty. Selfish beyond measure.

But not enough to stop.

She didn't want to think about the fact that she'd left her room after tossing and turning for hours, and despite what she might have let Hugo think, she knew that she hadn't been dressed like a governess should have been. Or even as a guest should have been when she'd eased her door open and crept down the hall. She been filled with a kind of despairing recklessness, a restless need that had urged her to *do something* with all the pent-up hurt and betrayal she'd felt after dinner. She'd convinced herself that it was an excellent idea to wander the halls of Groves House half-dressed. Hair down. Bare feet.

Had she wanted this all along?

But she didn't really care if she had, because it felt like dancing.

Hugo kissed her and he kissed her. His hands moved from the nape of her neck, smoothing their way down the line of her back, and fastened thrillingly at her hips, drawing her against him.

He kissed her as if there was nothing else but that. Nothing in all the world but the slide of his mouth on hers.

"I can't get enough of you," Hugo muttered against her lips, as if it hurt him to say that. "I can't get enough."

And when he bent, then lifted her into his arms, Eleanor knew she should have protested. Nothing had made this any less wrong than it had been yesterday. Or a week ago. Or ever. She was still his employee.

But he was Hugo Grovesmoor. And Vivi was right here, in this house, but he hadn't chosen her.

He'd chosen Eleanor. He'd called her beautiful and he'd kissed her, *after* meeting Vivi. After Vivi had launched a full-scale offensive, in fact, and gotten nowhere.

For the first time in her life, someone had chosen Eleanor.

She didn't have it in her to pull away.

Hugo carried her through the house. Eleanor had no concept of what time it was, only that the last time she'd heard the clocks chime, it had been after midnight. But as far she was concerned, the night could last forever. She hoped it would.

She rested her head against Hugo's wide shoulder, and let the house drift past her as he carried her. Through the halls and up the stairs that led to his private wing. And this time, he did not take her to his library, or to that dining room of his where she'd spent all evening feeling as if she didn't exist, but further on. Down to the end of that same hall, and into the rooms that waited there.

She had a dreamy sort of impression of magnificence. Bold, masculine furnishings, dark woods and impressively large paintings and rugs so lavish it seemed a shame to walk on them. A massive stone fireplace that made her think of medieval castles, and that was only the living room.

But Hugo kept going. And with every step he took toward what had to be his bedroom, Eleanor's heart kicked at her. Harder and harder.

And then they were there, standing by the side of a massive bed that would have dwarfed a room any smaller than this one, and Hugo was shifting her. Placing her down on the edge of his mattress as if she was infinitely precious to him.

And Eleanor felt shivery. Fragile all the way through.

Because she couldn't think of another time in her life that anyone had treated her like that, as if she mattered. Oh, she assumed her parents had. But the truth was that she couldn't remember any longer. What she remembered was taking care of others.

She tilted her face up, so she could study Hugo's gorgeously male expression—hungry and intense— as he gazed back at her. He made her feel like she was dancing even when she was still. He made her feel small in all the best ways.

The truth was that he made her feel like the kind of girl she'd never been. Light, airy. Charming beyond measure.

He made her feel the way she'd always imagined it felt to be Vivi.

Eleanor still couldn't believe that she was the one sitting here, on the edge of the Duke's bed. That he hadn't picked Vivi when he'd had the chance.

But she had no intention of throwing this away. This was her chance at last. To experience everything she never had before. To be that girl some part of her had always dreamed she could have been, maybe, if things had been different.

"I would tell you I don't bite, little one," Hugo said in that smokily amused way of his. It reverberated up and down her spine, then pooled somewhere low in her belly, where it began to pulse. "But that would be a lie."

"I'm not afraid of you," she managed to say.

Hugo looked amused. Something like delighted.

"No, you are not. And it is one among many reasons you are under my skin." He studied her. "But still, you're still looking at me as if you expect me to eat you alive."

"Oh," Eleanor said softly. "I thought that was exactly what you intended to do."

Hugo let out a breath. Or perhaps it was a laugh. Either way, it shimmered in Eleanor like light.

"You'll be the death of me," Hugo muttered.

And then he was moving. He hooked an arm around Eleanor's waist and hauled her along with him as he crawled toward the center of the bed. And then, marvelously, he stretched out on top of her and settled the whole of his lean, hard body between her legs.

"Breathe," he told her, and she knew she wasn't mistaking that unholy amusement in his dark gaze. His eyes looked even more like whiskey tonight, or perhaps it was just that this close, she couldn't pretend that she was anything but drunk.

On him.

"I'm breathing," she whispered.

"See that you continue," Hugo ordered her in his lazy, aristocratic way. "I haven't killed a virgin yet."

And Eleanor loved the fact that he knew. That she didn't have to make any long, drawn-out confession. When she'd thought about this moment—in those few and far between moments when she still imagined that this was any kind of possibility, that she might give herself to a man—she'd always assumed that she would have to offer extensive explanations. She would have to tell a reasonable story about why a woman her age had never quite managed to get here before, horizontal on a bed. She would have to talk about how distant she'd always felt from others her age, in part because she'd felt so responsible for Vivi, and how that had always seemed to leave her on her own. And she'd never been able to conjure up a way to tell someone that story without coming across as some kind of freak. Better to lock all that away. Better to convince herself that not only didn't she care, but she didn't feel the same things others did.

But Hugo didn't seem to care about any of that. Not why she was a virgin at twenty-seven. Not how. The only thing he seemed to care about was that he was the one braced over her, gazing down at her as if she was a treat. As if he wanted nothing more than to bury himself in her.

As if it was only a matter of time before he did.

It took Eleanor long moments to realize what that sensation was that snaked his way through her. A blistering sort of relief.

Because she felt safe. Somehow, someway, Hugo Grovesmoor made her feel safe, here in his bed where that should have been the very last thing she felt.

She hadn't known that was possible.

"Stop thinking so hard, little one," he said then.

"That's easy for you to say," she retorted. And his mouth was at her neck, so she felt it when he smiled.

"This is very simple," he told her, and there was a serious note beneath all that lazy heat. "If I want you to do something, I'll tell you what and how to do it. Otherwise, all you need to do is enjoy yourself."

Eleanor frowned at him, and he must have sensed it, because as he looked up that smile of his widened.

"That sounds very selfish."

"Eleanor, please." Hugo shook his head. "You cannot possibly be more selfish than I am. I promise you."

And then he put his mouth against her skin again, and Eleanor stopped thinking about anything.

Hugo took his time.

He tasted her everywhere. First he ran his hand over every part of her he could touch. He traced her collarbones. He tested her figure, spending a lot of time on her waist and the generous curves above and below. He made her writhe side to side beneath him, and when he had enough of that, he stripped her of her wrapper and her silky little nightie, and he did it all over again.

But this time, he used his mouth too.

He took her nipples in his mouth and sucked on them until she sobbed. He played with her. He made her arch up against him and cry out, over and over, and only when she felt limp and outside herself did he shift down the length of her body.

And then put his mouth between her legs.

Shattering the world into a white hot panic.

He licked into her. What he'd done with his fingers in the library had been astonishing enough, but this was worse. Better.

This was unlike anything Eleanor could possibly have imagined.

And when that wall came at her this time, she wasn't afraid of it. She let him throw her over the edge once, then again, and she shook and shimmered all the way down.

When she opened her eyes again, Hugo was naked too. And he was crawling his way over her again, his eyes locked to hers.

"You're holding up beautifully," he said, that curve in his lips. "I haven't even had to tell you to lie back and think of England."

"I always thought that would be unsanitary," she blurted out. That curve in his mouth bloomed into a real smile.

"You may well be the death of me, Eleanor. Here. Tonight."

"It always sounded so…" She trailed off, aftershocks still shuddering through her.

"It is *so*," Hugo told her. "That's what makes it so much fun."

And then Eleanor's attention was stolen away by the way Hugo settled himself against her once more.

And this time, she could feel everything.

That beautiful chest of his, chiseled and perfect and hot to the touch. But more than that, there was that heavy, foreign part of him that she could feel nudging up against the place where she was soft and melting. It made her shudder.

She reached down between them and wrapped her hand around him. His breath hissed out of him, hard. And there was that strange glitter in his eyes.

Eleanor pulled her hand away. Guiltily. "I'm sorry," she said hesitantly. "I didn't mean to hurt you."

"You didn't hurt me." Hugo's voice was strangled.

"I promise you, there's no possible way you could hurt me. But hold off on that for now."

Eleanor realized in the next instant what she'd done. She did read, after all. And she had certainly watched enough television in her time. But nothing had prepared her for how different it was in real life. Hugo was big and sculpted and stunning, and still he shuddered when she touched him. How could she have known? A thousand Hollywood movies were nothing next to the feel of his body above hers, and the way that silken length of his had burned itself into her palm.

Hugo shifted. She felt the tip of him nudge its way between the folds he'd licked, and then begin to move. Up and around. Nudging against the place that made her shiver the most, wilder and wilder each time.

"Will it hurt?" she asked.

Hugo's dark gaze glittered. "Hideously."

"Is that meant to be reassuring?" she asked him, and it was hard to catch her breath. But not because she was afraid of the potential pain.

"You strike me as a woman who appreciates the truth, Eleanor. Are you not?"

"Surely it can't be that bad or people wouldn't do it all the time."

"If you already know," Hugo drawled, "then why did you ask?"

Eleanor scowled at him. She opened up her mouth to snap something at him, and that was when he slid himself inside of her.

All the way inside of her.

Eleanor choked back whatever she might have been about to say. Pain lanced through her—

But it wasn't pain. In the next instant, she realized that it was sensation, certainly, and almost too much of it. Still, it wasn't *pain*.

It was somehow sharp and full at once. She felt exposed, even though Hugo covered the whole of her body with his. She felt shaky and taken, and still, somehow, fragile and precious at once.

"Did it hurt?" Hugo asked, his voice little more than a growl.

Eleanor tested it. She shifted her hips a little bit this way, then that. Then again.

And each time she moved, the sensation changed. The fullness remained, but the sharpness eased. Until she started to suspect that the fullness was warmth. She tried it again, and again, and sure enough the more she moved, the warmer it got.

And it spiraled out from that place inside her, and set the rest of her on fire.

"Hideously," she whispered up at him.

Hugo grinned. And then he began to move.

And Eleanor understood that she'd only known sparks.

This was the fire.

Hugo was thorough. He set a slow, easy pace, and Eleanor met it as she wrapped herself around him. And then she mirrored him. She did what he did.

He put his mouth on her skin and she returned the favor. When he thrust deep into her, she lifted her hips to meet each stroke. And the more she did it, the less smooth and studied he became.

Until he seemed as out of breath and outside himself as she was.

Something cracked wide open inside of her. She felt it happen as he slammed into her, sending that impossible joy dancing all through her veins.

"What the hell you doing to me?" Hugo whispered fiercely, his face in the crook of her neck.

And that crack only widened further, and filled with light.

He'd chosen her. And here, beneath him, with him deep inside of her and everything fire and need and all that beautiful hunger, she couldn't help but believe that maybe he needed her, too.

Not because she was a woman to scratch some itch. He was Hugo Grovesmoor. He could have any woman he liked for that kind of thing, she knew that. But because she was her, specifically.

Because together, they were *them*.

And that was more precious than anything, even all the priceless things cluttering up this rambling old house.

With every deep stroke, every life-altering thrust, she believed it more.

And when she found herself falling this time, cracked wide open and full of him, it felt like love.

Especially when Hugo followed her over, shouting out her name.

CHAPTER ELEVEN

It was very early the next morning when Eleanor finally slipped from Hugo's bed, placing her unsteady feet on the floor beside the massive bed where she'd slept in snatches and learned a whole lot of things about pleasure.

Dark, delirious, wondrous things that still moved in her, making her flush hot and red all over again, just remembering.

She ached everywhere, she realized as she stood. Places she'd had no idea *could* ache were half on fire, making her feel as if she'd woken up in someone else's body. There were tugs here and vague abrasions there, and she could remember something wild and carnal and inexpressibly beautiful to explain each one.

Eleanor thought she ought to be ashamed. Maybe she would be, later. When the reality of last night had time to settle. But right here, right now, she didn't regret a thing.

She found the nightclothes she'd worn last night and pulled them back on, trying hard not to remember exactly how Hugo had pulled each of them off her. Trying hard not to slip off into that same red haze again, all flushed and needy.

She peeked over her shoulder at the bed again, some part of her still unable to believe that any of this had happened. One red-hot image after the next chased itself through her head, in case her body couldn't tell her what had happened, inside and out. But if she'd had any lingering doubt, the sight of Hugo sprawled out there across the better part of his bed got rid of it.

She had tasted every inch of him. She'd taken that enormous length of his deep into her mouth, and had learned how to taste him and tease him the way he'd done to her. He'd taught her how to kneel up over him, and had taken her that way. He'd taught her all the wicked things he could do with his hands, and she'd tried to do the same to him. Over and over again.

She had no idea there were so many different ways—an infinite number of ways, apparently—to do the same thing. Crack apart like that and fall together, sleep entangled, then wake to do it again.

And the greedy part of her wanted to experience all of them. Every last possible way to explode like that. Here and now, though she was a little bit stiff and still achey. Eleanor didn't care, as long she got to experience it all with Hugo.

Hugo, who lay on his back with his arms splayed wide, as commanding in his bed as he was out of it. Hugo, who looked more approachable when she slept.

No smirking. No mocking tone of voice. No reminders that he considered himself the biggest monster in England, because everyone else did.

Everyone except Eleanor, that was.

She tucked her hair behind her ears and forced herself to turn around. To walk toward the bedroom door, and then, harder still, to walk out and leave Hugo there behind her when that was the last thing she wanted to do.

Because whatever else happened, she had a job to do. A little girl who had enough of people in her life abandoning her in one way or another, and didn't need more of that from Eleanor.

And if there was a part of her that didn't want to be there when Hugo woke, well. She told herself that was nothing but her inbred practicality. The man might not have had the relationship everyone thought he'd had with Isobel Vanderhaven, but that didn't mean he been a saint.

Eleanor refused to be that silly virgin she'd certainly read enough about and seen too many times on-screen. The one who fell head over heels at the first hint of a man's interest and made a complete fool of herself.

There wasn't much she could do about the first part of that, but she'd be damned if she'd make a fool of herself. Not if she could avoid it.

Once outside of Hugo's rooms, she ducked her head down and moved as quickly as she could through the house without actually breaking into a run. It was still early, so she thought it was likely that no one would be up and around yet. Even so, she took the back stairs whenever possible, the better to be sure no one saw her wandering around, so far from her own rooms, in her revealing sleepwear.

"Better safe than sorry," she muttered to herself.

And then she let out a huge sigh of relief when she made it to her door. All she could think about, then, was that enormous tub in her bathroom and slipping her whole, sweetly aching body into the deep embrace of it. She pushed her way through the door, already piling her hair on the top of her head in anticipation.

"Where have you been?"

Eleanor flinched at the sound of that voice. It startled her so badly that it took her longer than it should have to realize that it was Vivi, of course. Because who else could it be?

She dropped her arms, the hair she hadn't quite managed to put into a knot tumbling down around her shoulders, and she told herself she had no reason whatsoever to feel guilty. About anything.

And yet that was exactly what she felt as she found her sister standing there in the doorway to the bedroom, her arms crossed and a flat sort of look on her face.

For a moment, they stared at each other across the stillness of the early morning.

"Sometimes when I can't sleep," Eleanor said with as much quiet dignity as she could manage, "I walk in the halls. It gets the blood moving, at the very least."

Vivi let out a small sort of laugh that suggested she didn't find anything funny at all.

"You can't possibly expect me to believe that, can you? I'm your sister, not your seven-year-old student."

"What are you doing here, Vivi?" Eleanor asked softly. "The guest suites are clear across the house."

Vivi's mouth was a taut line, and that flat look was still making her new gold eyes look a bit more tarnished than usual. "I went looking for you. I was after a little bit of sister time. And guess what? You haven't been here for hours."

"You wanted sister time in the middle of the night?" Eleanor asked, and she didn't try too hard to keep the skepticism out of her voice. "Did you imagine that I would be awake? Or did you think you would wake me up, even though I have to get up and work in the morning?"

Neither one, she was well aware, said great things about how her sister saw her. Hugo's words swirled around in her head, and it seemed she couldn't banish them the way she wished she could. And something sour was sloshing around in her belly, making it worse.

Because Eleanor didn't know that it would really be all that out of line if Vivi *had* assumed that Eleanor would be perfectly all right with being woken up at all hours. Wasn't that what her role had always been? And there was only one person who had demanded Eleanor stay in that role. Eleanor herself.

She had always been so desperate to be needed,

because love was tricky and people died and took their love with them. Need was better. Need made her indispensable.

But it had never made her feel as alive as Hugo had. As if she'd been sleepwalking for years.

"Do you think I can't tell what you've been up to?" Vivi asked. Her voice was strange. As flat as her gaze, and yet there was that sharp undercurrent. "How could you do this?"

"I don't know what you think I've done." Eleanor squared her shoulders and forced herself to ignore the part of her that had always been afraid to square off with Vivi. Because if she lost Vivi on top of everything else she'd lost, what would she have? She clarified. "To you."

Vivi shook her head. "All the things I've done, all the trouble I've gone to for *us*, Eleanor. And you can't even tell me the truth."

"I think that's unfair."

"If you had something going on with the Duke, you should have told me, so I wouldn't have bothered making a fool of myself at that dinner last night." Vivi shook her head. "Am I just a party trick you like to trot out to amuse yourself and your aristocratic friend?"

The sweeping injustice of that was almost enough to knock Eleanor back a step or two.

"I don't have any 'aristocratic friends,' Vivi," Eleanor managed to say, her voice on the verge of trembling. It felt a lot like anger, something she'd always swallowed down before. Something she'd always pretended she didn't feel, no matter what. "I think we both know that's you, not me. I work at Groves House. You're on holiday. It's been years since we decided it would make sense for you to make like a socialite and land a rich husband, and all you've done since is go to parties and spend the money I make. Which one of us is the party trick?"

She heard her own words hanging there in the quiet of the room, and could feel them shaking around inside of her, like a new kind of shivering. And she didn't know if she needed to lie down. Or possibly get sick. Or apologize, instantly.

But she didn't do any of those things. She should have said something years ago. She'd bitten her tongue and she'd bitten her tongue—and it was funny, wasn't it, that it took Hugo teaching her all the other, more fun things she could do with it to loosen it at last.

Eleanor waited to feel shamed by that, but it didn't come.

"This is why they call him a monster," Vivi said softly. "You know that, right? He ruins everything he touches. Even us."

Abruptly, Eleanor was finished with this conversation. She'd had enough. She straightened herself up and reminded herself that she was a grown woman. Not a teen who'd been caught sneaking about after curfew. She didn't have to stand here and offer explanations.

And she certainly didn't need to listen to her sister's malicious and uninformed thoughts about Hugo.

"I don't need an interrogation, Vivi," she said then. Not unkindly. Just matter-of-factly. "I really do have to work in a couple of hours."

"You can't possibly think—" Vivi began, a scornful sort of note in her voice that Eleanor didn't like at all.

"I don't ask you to account for yourself, do I?" she retorted, cutting Vivi off as she moved across the floor toward the doorway her sister stood in. "I choose to believe that everything you do, you do with both our best interests at heart. I don't understand why you can't extend me the same courtesy."

She brushed past Vivi then, half expecting her sister to grab her arm and escalate things the way she'd been known to do in the past, but Vivi only watched her—closely—as she made her way into the bathroom. Eleanor turned on the taps, ran her fingers through the water as she fiddled with the temperature, and pretended everything was normal. That she was still a virgin. That she was still the same person she'd been yesterday.

That she hadn't spent her night so full of Hugo in every possible way that she could barely breathe now.

The truth was, she didn't want to breathe.

And love her sister as she might, she didn't want to share what had happened with her. Eleanor wanted to keep it to herself. She wanted to hold it tight.

She wanted to hoard it, a bright, gleaming evening set against the rest of her practical life.

"He will chew you up and spit you out," Vivi said

darkly from the door. "That's what he does, like it's his job. Because he doesn't have a real job."

Eleanor shook the water off her hand as she straightened. There were so many things she could say to that. For example, she could point out that Vivi had dressed for dinner last night as if she was perfectly willing to risk a few tooth marks. But she didn't. She only walked to the bathroom door and she smiled at her sister.

"Are you concerned for me?" she asked quietly. "Or is this something else?"

Vivi flushed at that. Her eyes narrowed. "Of course I'm concerned for you. What else would it be?"

"I can't imagine."

"I'm not jealous of you, Eleanor, if that's what you mean."

"Perish the thought," Eleanor said dryly.

"The truth is, I know what men like Hugo Grovesmoor are like. You don't. I've spent years around his type while you've…"

"Yes." Eleanor nodded. "While I've scuttled about in the shadows like the help."

Vivi let out a breath, and if Eleanor wasn't mistaken, the look in her new gold eyes then was pity.

Something in her froze solid.

"If you don't like your life, you should change it," Vivi said quietly. "I'll help. But Hugo Grovesmoor isn't a change, Eleanor. He's an atom bomb. And I understand that you're hopped up on hormones right now and feeling lavish, but I don't think you're prepared for the damage a man like him will do."

"I love you, Vivi," Eleanor managed to say past the sudden, sinking feeling inside of her, because who was she kidding? She knew nothing about men, much less men like Hugo. Why was she so certain she was right and Vivi was wrong? "You know I do. But I have to get ready for my day."

"I love you, too," Vivi retorted. "And don't worry. I'm going to prove it. I'll take care of you. I always said I would."

Eleanor didn't know what that meant and more, she was certain she didn't want to know, especially once Vivi left.

She ran her bath and she sat in it for a long time, until the water grew cold and the clock in her living room told her it was time to move. Then she climbed out, toweled off, and got dressed for her usual day with Geraldine as if she was still the same old Eleanor in the same old body she'd had before.

Because she was, damn it. No atom bombs. No damage.

She was exactly who she'd always been, despite her ill-considered words to Vivi. She castigated herself for each and every one of them as she took Geraldine through her lessons, the last she'd have for a few days now that Eleanor's initial six weeks were up and Eleanor was due a brief holiday. They talked about what Geraldine would do over her break. They talked about the books Geraldine was reading and

Geraldine's many adventures with Pono, the rooster plush toy she liked best.

They did not see the Duke. Eleanor told herself she was grateful. Because she didn't want to be that silly virgin—the one even her own sister seemed certain she already was—and that meant she'd needed the day to regain her equanimity.

"You're fine now," she told herself stoutly as she climbed the stairs from the nursery that led to her rooms. "Perfectly fine, as ever."

But when she let herself into her rooms, Vivi was waiting. Again.

"You should have just had a cot brought in," Eleanor said mildly.

"I think you'd better pack, love," Vivi replied. "We'll need to leave tonight."

"No need for that, surely," Eleanor said. She sank down on the nearest upright, Elizabethan chair. "We can leave in the morning. More chance of a train, I'd think."

"You don't understand," Vivi said, and while her voice was patient, her gaze was not. Her eyes fairly danced, too bright and a bit too sharp, as if she'd been at the spirits again. "You're not going to want to be here in the morning."

Eleanor discovered that she was tired. Very, very tired. That was what happened when a person got all of about twelve minutes of sleep all night long. She couldn't say she regretted it. But it had obviously dulled her brain, because she wasn't following Vivi at all.

"Vivi," she began, "I really don't…"

"I told you I would take care of you and I meant it," her sister said stoutly. "There are certain tabloids that are so desperate for a story about Hugo that they'd pay anything for a fake one. Which means they'd pay twice that for a real one."

Eleanor was glad she was sitting down, because she thought that if she hadn't been, she might have fallen.

"No," she managed to say from a far distance, while her ears buzzed at her and her lunch threatened the back of her throat. "I signed a nondisclosure agreement. I can't sell anything."

"You can't," Vivi said with a hard sort of shrug. "But I can. There's been nothing new on Hugo in ages. Everyone's tired of speculating what horrors he's visiting on that poor kid. A sex romp with the governess is exactly what they'd expect, isn't it?"

"I forbid it," Eleanor snapped, and she hardly recognized her own voice. Or the fact she'd surged to her feet and had balled her hands up into fists.

Vivi only eyed her from across the room, that pitying look on her face again.

"I thought you'd say something like that."

"You thought correctly."

"Which is why I didn't consult you." Vivi shook her head. "It's done, Eleanor. We have five hundred thousand pounds in our account and you don't have to say a word. Or do another thing. Our troubles are over. But the story is running tomorrow." Vivi tilted her head, taking in the house all around them.

This life Eleanor had known better than to get too attached to—hadn't she? And Hugo, whose name seemed to detonate inside of her, shaking through her. Shaking her. "And if I were you, I wouldn't be here when he reads it."

CHAPTER TWELVE

ELEANOR HAD BETRAYED HIM.

What bothered Hugo most was that somehow, this entirely predictable turn of events surprised him.

"Off to catch the last train," Mrs. Redding had said yesterday afternoon when Hugo had actually lowered himself to ask where Eleanor was, with her usual disapproving sniff. "A bit keen to celebrate her time off, if you ask me."

"No one did," Hugo had replied, with a smile. A cheeky one. Which had done absolutely nothing but make the old woman roll her eyes. Their love language, he'd told himself.

But that had been before the tabloids published their usual filth and innuendo in the morning. That had been when he was still looking forward to seeing her. Craving it, if he was honest. He'd woken yesterday morning to find her missing from his bed and it was as if he was missing a limb. As if they'd spent every night of a good five years sleeping wrapped around each other in the same bed, and her sudden absence hurt.

Hurt.

He didn't understand it. Or perhaps he didn't want to understand it. Yesterday, all he'd wanted was to lose himself in her innocence. Her sweetness. And all that intoxicating heat.

Somehow he'd forgotten to be cynical where Eleanor was concerned.

An unforgivable oversight.

Because sometime yesterday, when he'd still been lying in his bed surrounded by her scent and marveling at the notion that innocence could be so addictive—transformative, even, which should have appalled someone as calcified in his own bitterness as Hugo had been for years—Eleanor had not been doing the same. Instead, she had been sharing what had happened between them with her sister. Reporting back, perhaps, that their plan had worked? And sometimes after that, Vivi had sold an extraordinarily salacious and sordid tale to the most shrill and suggestive of the tabloids about *Horrible Hugo*, the *Most Hated Duke in England*, and his *Sexcapades with his Governesses*.

Really, Hugo could have written it himself.

What astonished him was that he hadn't. He'd let his guard down for the first time since Isobel had gotten her hooks in him—hell, he'd even told Eleanor the truth. As if she was someone he could trust. As if, when she'd sounded so appalled at the very notion that anyone could sell him out to the tabloids, she'd meant it.

Hugo couldn't trust anyone. Ever. How many times did he need to learn it?

The truth was, he'd handed Eleanor and her sister all the ammunition they'd need. Fourteen previous governesses, all unceremoniously sacked. When the suspiciously unknown sister of a periodic tabloid bit of arm candy, the overly ambitious Vivi—whose desperation repeatedly led her to all sorts of entanglements that found their way into tawdry little tell-alls—had turned up, Hugo should have seen this coming.

Why hadn't he seen this coming?

Hugo treats his governesses like his own private harem!

That was what the paper screeched, in that awful tone they used when they were putting words into people's mouths. Then again, he imagined a woman who could giggle aggressively the way Vivi Andrews had could turn a pointed phrase or two when she had a mind to.

He doesn't give a toss about poor Isobel's baby, preferring depraved sex romps in his country estate to changing nappies.

It was nothing he hadn't read before a thousand times. It wasn't even particularly well done, in his opinion, given he was now a kind of connoisseur of tabloid hit pieces. A giant spread with vague accusations about unsavory sexual practices, a glamour shot of Vivi as if she was the governess in question next to a picture of what might have been Eleanor in a hooded something or other, and an excuse to fling pictures of lost, sainted Isobel and Torquil all over the place. Along with everyone's favorite picture of toddler Geraldine—all gap teeth and copper curls, looking lost and in need of nappy-changing—as if she'd been preserved forever at an age when Hugo's neglect could have resulted in her toddling about in her own filth.

He was tempted to ring up Vivi Andrews himself and demand a cut of what must have been a very tidy profit. But he couldn't do that, could he, because that would mean very coldly and calculatedly discussing when and how Vivi and her sister had decided to set him up so beautifully.

And then asking the question he wanted to know the answer to but was afraid to ask: How had they known that Eleanor's brand of stroppy innocence would send him crashing to his knees? He'd had women throwing themselves at him his entire life. Some were desperate for the title. Others only wanted a little turn in the tabloids. He'd have said that there was no possible approach he hadn't grown tired of years ago.

But somehow they'd picked the one that worked.

He had a lot of questions for Eleanor. He was even tempted to question whether her virginity had been real—but no. He knew better. He'd been there. The betrayal was real, but so was that night. So was what had passed between them.

Hugo might not know much, but he knew that.

Not that it helped. He still found himself stalking around his damned house in the gloomy twilight, like a sepulchral poet or something equally tragic.

Hugo couldn't remember the last time he'd surrendered so completely to self-pity. He made his lonely, nauseatingly melancholic way into his library, broodingly eyeing the shelves he'd once told Eleanor she'd nearly knocked down. Tonight he was tempted to knock them down himself. With a bottle of whiskey and his own hard head.

Because he never learned.

He was the monster of all of England's most fervent fantasies, paying out his penance in his rambling out house, alone. Forever.

Nothing could change that. Not his own disinterest in the narrative. Not the fact his ward was, despite all wailing to the contrary, a healthy and relatively happy child. Not a scowling, insufficiently respectful governess who'd treated him as an irritant to be borne, much like the sulky moors all around.

He might have imagined that things had changed that night and that wildly optimistic morning after, but that was only more proof that he was an idiot of epic proportions.

"Nothing new in that," he muttered to himself, not even bothering to scowl at the fire. "It's the bloody story of my life."

As was the certainty that somehow, he would pay for this, too.

The door to the library opened then. Hugo watched, bemused, as it scraped its way inward across the thick rug on the floor. Almost as if the person entering the room wasn't strong enough to move it.

He blinked when he saw the figure standing in the door then. It was Geraldine, who never sought him out of her own accord, and never here. She usually suffered warily through her dinners with him, eyeing him suspiciously from her place down the table. Tonight she looked less like the celebrated daughter of a world-renowned beauty and more…like a kid. Her copper-colored plaits stood out at odd angles from her head, she was dressed in a jumper and jeans like any random child might have been, and her little face was drawn into a frown.

She looked sturdy. And surly, Hugo couldn't help but notice.

"Yes, my ward?" he drawled. He lounged back in his chair before the fire and raised his brows at her, doing his best, as ever, to sound like a proper guardian instead of the world's favorite scandal.

The little girl screwed up her nose while the corners of her pudgy mouth turned down, but she kept her scowl aimed right at him.

Evidence of Eleanor's teaching, clearly, he thought, and hated the lancing sensation of something that couldn't be pain—because he refused to accept pain—straight through him.

"Nanny Marie says Miss Andrews is never coming back."

Hugo waited for her to continue, but Geraldine only stared at him. Rather challengingly, actually.

"I am at a loss as to where *Nanny Marie*," and he utterly failed to keep the sardonic inflection from his tone at that name, "would get the impression that she has access to staffing decisions."

"I like her."

"Nanny Marie? I couldn't identify her in a lineup, I'm afraid. Much less determine whether or not I cared for her one way or another."

"Miss Andrews."

Geraldine sounded testy, but definitive. And that was the trouble. Hugo liked Miss Andrews, too. Definitively.

Even now.

He'd told Eleanor things he'd never told anyone. He'd expected her to understand him when no one else had, ever. And then sure enough, she had. Meanwhile, she'd held on to her innocence far, far longer than most women her age, and she'd gifted it to him. *Him.* As if it had never occurred to her that Hugo the Horrible wasn't a suitable recipient for such a gift.

As if she'd felt completely safe with him, which should have been impossible.

And as if that wasn't enough, Hugo wasn't entirely sure that she was the one who had been rendered fragile by what had happened that night. There were parts of him that no longer fit the way they had before. Parts of him that scraped at all the walls he'd built inside, as if *he* didn't fit anymore.

He had been perfectly content here. Happy enough to live out the consequences of Isobel's decisions far away from prying eyes and telescopic lenses. Perfectly willing to let the country shake in horror at the notion of what he might be doing to their lost saint's precious little girl. No small part of him had thrilled to the idea that he was literally some people's nightmare. Every single night.

He'd taken pleasure in that. They deserved it.

Hugo couldn't understand where all that had gone. How it had disappeared in the course of one very long, very thorough exploration of a prim governess's astonishingly curvy body.

What was it in him that couldn't shrug her off the way he had all the others? Why was it so impossible to draw a line under the latest tabloid scandal and move on? When his past mistakes had aired out his laundry in front of whole nations, Hugo had been unbothered.

He had the sinking, lowering notion that all this time, he'd never known real ruin at all.

"You didn't fire her, did you?" Geraldine demanded, reminding him he was not alone with his brooding.

Hugo eyed her. The little girl had moved further into the room. Now she stood near the fireplace, her hands on her little hips, glaring at her guardian without a seeming care in the world. As if she thought, should there be an altercation, she could take him.

He had tried so hard these past three years, since the accident that had taken Isobel and Torquil. He'd kept his distance from this child. He had tended to Geraldine's needs, but not in a way that could ever hurt her. Or compromise her. He'd been certain—as certain as his critics, if not more so—that left to his own devices, he could only do harm.

That was what he did, he knew. Harm.

He certainly hadn't allowed himself to like Geraldine. Or anyone.

But all he could see was Eleanor, then. Her face, so lovely and so fierce, as she'd stood up for Geraldine. *It's not her fault,* she'd told him.

And Hugo knew that. He'd gone out of his way to make sure he never brought his feelings about Isobel into any interaction he had with Geraldine. But it hadn't occurred to him until today—until Eleanor—that he hadn't let his feelings enter into anything in a very long time.

Because the fact of the matter was, he rather liked this little girl. He liked how unafraid she was. He liked the fact that she was seven years old and yet had no apparent second thoughts about walking straight into her guardian's library and confronting him. And the more he stared at her, the less she seemed to care. Her little chin tilted up. She even sniffed, as if impatient.

She was a fighter. How could he not adore her for it?

Especially when he'd stopped fighting so long ago.

"If I did fire her, that would be my decision as your

guardian and would not require a consultation, Geraldine," Hugo said reprovingly. But when her face looked stormy, he relented. "But I didn't let her go."

He crooked his finger and then pointed to the leather chair across from him. Geraldine made a huffing sound that did not bode well for her teen years, but she obeyed him. With perhaps a little too much stomping, and more attitude than he would have thought possible from a sweet little child, she moved from the fireplace to climb up into the big leather chair. The big piece of furniture seemed to swallow her whole, but that didn't bother Geraldine. She slid back, stuck her feet out straight in front of her, and crossed her arms over her chest.

Mutinously.

"Where is she if you didn't get rid of her?" Geraldine asked as if she'd caught Hugo out in a dirty lie.

"I feel certain Miss Andrews told you that she was taking a few days' break. She does get one, you know. We can't lock her away in a cage and force her to stay here all the time."

Though the idea held some appeal.

The little girl's chin jutted out. "Why not?"

"Excellent question."

"We should go get her back, then," Geraldine said, with a wide gesture of one hand, as if Hugo really was an idiot and she was leading him to the right answer because he was taking too long to get there himself.

And the damnedest thing was, Hugo admired that, too.

Geraldine was not yet ten and yet she was showing more fight than he had in the past fifteen years.

Why had he allowed Isobel to paint him the way she had? Of course there was no fighting a slanted story or a nasty rumor, but he hadn't tried and he hadn't done anything else, either. He hadn't pointedly lived a life completely opposed to the one Isobel claimed he did. He'd never even defended himself. He'd told himself it was because he was too proud to dignify her claims with a response, but was that truly it? Or was it the same sort of martyrdom he'd always abhorred when Isobel faked it?

Had he been waiting all this time for someone to look at him and see him and believe that he wasn't the things that had been said about him?

Maybe there was some virtue in that. Or there could have been—had his father not died believing the very worst of him.

The fact of the matter was, Hugo had never seen the point of fighting battles he'd decided in advance that he couldn't win. He'd never righted a single wrong. He'd simply sat here and taken it. And to what end?

Whether the public loved him or hated him, he was the only parental influence in this child's life. And despite that handicap, Geraldine appeared to be thriving. She was flushed with indignation, and if he wasn't mistaken, love.

Love.

It thudded into him. Then again. Like another

fight he was destined to lose. But this time, he didn't intend to go down alone.

Was it virtue to act as if he was a punching bag for all these years or was it an especially noxious version of self-pity?

Hugo didn't know. But he did know this. He was a creature of temper and mood, unable to control himself at any time, the tabloids said.

So he saw no reason to start now.

"Yes," he said slowly, smiling at Geraldine. Until she smiled back, as if they were together in this. Because they were. "We really should get her back. What an excellent idea."

CHAPTER THIRTEEN

RETURNING TO LONDON was like being slapped in the face with the pitiless palm of a little too much reality. But there was nothing to do but grin and bear it.

Eleanor gritted her teeth, figuratively and literally, and set about cleaning up Vivi's mess.

Not the big mess, of course. Not the mess that haunted her, making her feel sick and small and ashamed. Or shaky every time she saw the *Daily Mail* in a newsstand. Not the mess that rolled around inside of her, making her feel as oily and greasy and horrid as what Vivi had done, every time she drew breath—

No, there was no fixing that. Vivi had sold Eleanor's story as her own and asserted, repeatedly and proudly, that she would do it again. She claimed it was for both of their own good, though that prickly, ugly thing inside of Eleanor thought different and left marks every time it did. But it made no difference. It was done.

And Eleanor was just one more scar Hugo would add to his collection. One more lie to add to the rest.

Eleanor concentrated on the things she could fix.

She placated their landlord, pleading their case as sweetly as she could. She did not take Vivi's advice to simply tell the suspicious old woman where she could stuff it, because all that money that Vivi had been promised had yet to come through. She cleaned. Everything. From what passed for baseboards in their tiny tip of a flat to the windows and back. She cleaned every cup and saucer, plate and utensil. She even cleaned out the terrifying old tea mugs, coated in tannins as evidence of their long years of use.

She cleaned as if she was on a mission.

As if it was penance.

And none of that seemed to do a single thing to make her feel better.

Eleanor suspected that there would be no feeling better. That there would be no recovering from this. It didn't matter how she'd come to betray Hugo, surely. It only mattered that she had. Not only had she betrayed him, she hadn't even had the decency to look him in the face and let him know she'd done it.

She hadn't even said goodbye.

Instead, she'd snuck off into the gathering fall evening with her case and her sister, like some kind of thief in reverse.

That was the part she didn't think she could live with. That was the part that scraped to her belly like some ravenous beast with sharp claws. Over and over again.

"You're being a bit dramatic, no?" Vivi asked one evening.

The way she had back in that other life, when Eleanor had never met Hugo Grovesmoor and hadn't had the faintest idea how he would upend her life. The way she did with a little too much frequency, to Eleanor's mind, given her penchant for making an opera out of all and sundry.

Eleanor eyed her sister over the pile of mending that she'd been ruthlessly going through for days now that the flat fairly sparkled. Vivi's trousers. Vivi's poncey skirts. Vivi's lovely and expensive clothes that Vivi herself didn't bother to treat with anything resembling reverence. Or even the bare minimum of care, it appeared.

"While tending to your sewing?" Eleanor asked mildly, which was getting harder to do all the time. "I didn't realize it was possible to be theatrical while mending."

Vivi lifted herself up from the bit of floor in front of the telly, where she'd been flinging herself this way and that to a DVD of some shiny-toothed and alarmingly narrow American celebrity trainer.

"Everyone's obsessed with this workout," she'd informed Eleanor as she'd contorted about.

Eleanor had responded by finishing off the last packet of chocolate biscuits. *At* her.

Now Vivi plunked herself down on the small sofa next to Eleanor, making the cushion dip alarmingly and a pile of her waiting mending tip over. Eleanor thought she'd switch the telly over to a show and drown her mood out, as she been doing since they'd returned, but instead she twisted her body around so she could look her sister straight in the face.

"I know you think you hate me," Vivi said, her voice serious and an unexpected wallop. "I understand that. I even accept it. You don't have any experience with these things."

Eleanor's teeth ached. She made herself unclench her jaw.

"If you mean making up tawdry stories and selling them to the highest bidder, then no. I certainly don't."

"I mean Hugo." Vivi's voice was soft. Worse, kind. "I mean men."

Eleanor bent her head to the blouse she was attempting to repair. She kept her attention furiously focused on her needle. But she was sure that it was no use, that Vivi could see the flush that crept up the back of her neck and threatened her cheeks as well. She didn't understand how a topic that she'd been so pleased to discuss with Hugo—or not discuss, as the case might be, because he'd known and he'd handled it—she had no desire at all to discuss with her sister.

"I think I'd prefer to skip the 'poor, sad Eleanor' discussion tonight, thanks." Eleanor had to order herself to unclench her jaw. Again. And do something with her shoulders before she lifted them over the top of her head. "I think it's possible that the only thing worse than the story you sold might be your pity."

"I don't pity you, Eleanor," Vivi said, and her

voice was different. Almost unrecognizable. It made Eleanor uneasy. "I envy you. I don't think I've ever been soft or dewy-eyed about anything. Not even way back when you cried over me in the hospital and I didn't."

Eleanor paused. She very carefully put down her sewing. And then she turned and held her sister's gaze.

"Vivi. Please tell me you're not about to give me 'the talk.'"

Vivi's eyes gleamed then, and they really did look like shiny gold coins, something that Eleanor wished she could find more annoying than she did.

"You spent all night with Hugo Grovesmoor. I think any attempt at a sex talk at this point would be a waste of breath, don't you?"

Eleanor tried to hide the pain that flashed over her. Or that near-reflexive urge to draw in a sharp breath, as if that would ease it.

"I don't want to talk about Hugo."

It was more that she didn't want to talk about Hugo with Vivi, if she was honest. But either way, thinking about him was painful enough.

"I know you're not going to believe me." Vivi reached over and put her hand on Eleanor's leg, and all Eleanor could seem to do was stare at it. "I know that I'm too selfish and take you for granted and anything else you want to accuse me of. It's all true. I know it's true. But that doesn't mean I don't love you, Eleanor. And I get to protect you, too."

Eleanor frowned at that hand on her leg. Hard.

"Is that what you were doing, Vivi? Protecting me? Are you sure?"

Eleanor didn't know how she dared ask that—especially because she wasn't sure she wanted to know the answer. Beside her, Vivi blew out a breath. And when Eleanor looked up, something else glittered in her gaze.

"That's fair enough. I can't deny that I reacted a bit poorly when I arrived at Groves House. I guess it all took me by surprise."

"You were jealous." Eleanor held her sister's gaze, and dared her to refute it.

But Vivi only shrugged, making the curls she'd piled on the top of her head bob a bit. "I don't know what I was. I've worked hard, for years."

Eleanor wanted to argue that, but something made her hold her tongue. Vivi's gaze darkened.

"I've put up with people you wouldn't tolerate for the length of a simple conversation, thank you. I thought we were on the same page. I thought we had specific roles to play. And then it looked as if maybe everything I was doing was beside the point and I didn't know how to handle that." She shook her head. "I'm sorry I'm not as perfect as you are."

"That's not fair."

"You could have told me how much you liked him." Vivi's voice cracked slightly, startling them both. "You could have told me that, Eleanor."

"I didn't think you would have listened if I had."

Vivi shook her head, as if that had hurt her and she was reeling. "Of course I would have listened.

You're my sister. It's you and me against the world, remember?"

"I remember," Eleanor whispered. "Of course I remember."

They sat there for a moment, and something shifted inside of Eleanor as they did. That ugly, clawed weight seemed to dissipate a little.

"But this is what I wanted to talk to you about even if it makes you turn red. You don't know about men like Hugo, Eleanor. I do."

"I was under the impression that there were no men like Hugo."

She knew that was true for her. She thought it might also be true for the world, given the way they talked about him as if he'd rounded them all up, abused them horribly and personally, and then booted them out of a speeding vehicle.

"Men are more alike than not." And there was a weariness in Vivi's voice that pricked at Eleanor. She'd been so concentrated on herself. So focused on all the ways she felt overlooked. Taken advantage of. Why had it never occurred to her to wonder if her sister felt the same way? "Keen to take what they can get. No matter what. But it doesn't necessarily mean more than that."

And Eleanor wanted to argue. She wanted to tell Vivi that she was wrong. That she didn't know Hugo. But the fact was… Neither did Eleanor. She'd lived in his house, true. He'd flirted with her, she'd given him her virginity—but despite what that meant to her, it was likely all in a day's work for the likes of Hugo.

She believed that he wasn't the monster the tabloids had made him out to be. But that didn't make him a monk. It didn't make her any less of a fool. She felt her eyes fill up, and ducked her head to hide it. And blink the tears back before they could fall.

"I feel like such a fool," she whispered.

"I can't think of a woman who wouldn't fall for Hugo Grovesmoor," Vivi said, distinctly. "Not one. He's gorgeous and evil and everyone knows he's wild in bed. You never stood a chance."

She could talk about more of this than she'd thought, it turned out. But she couldn't talk about Hugo's reputation in bed. There was only so much she could be expected to handle, surely. Without cracking apart into little pieces, all over the floor, that she knew her careless sister would never sweep up.

"And what now?" Eleanor asked instead, lifting up her hands and then letting them drop back to her lap. "What am I supposed to do now?" She moved one hand in a lazy, circular motion that encompassed the whole of her chest. "With all of *this*."

Vivi laughed, then. It was that merry laugh of hers that still warmed up the room. It astonished Eleanor how welcoming she found the sound.

"That I can help with." Vivi got to her feet and reached out her hand, beckoning for Eleanor to join her. "Come on, then. The night is young and filled with trouble for us to throw ourselves into."

"Oh, no," Eleanor said then, with a frown. "I don't get into trouble. I—"

"You don't have a job that you have to go to bed early for. You have nowhere to be in the morning."

"Well—"

"And unless I'm mistaken, you're a bit of a scarlet woman, fresh from a shocking affair with the most hated man in England."

"But it's a Wednesday," Eleanor said. Scandalized.

"Ah, grasshopper," Vivi replied mischievously. "I have so much to teach you."

And that was how Eleanor found herself out at one of those desperately chic clubs that Vivi spent so much of her time in. This one was so new it was considered a coup to get in, Vivi informed Eleanor as she got them waved past the line that snaked off down the block and around the corner. On a blustery Wednesday.

Inside, it was a cavernous place, filled with too many dizzying lights and far too many people dressed sleek and sharp. Not exactly the sort of crowd Eleanor felt at home in. But Vivi had asked Eleanor to trust that she knew what she was doing, and Eleanor had agreed to do it.

That was how she'd ended up in the ridiculous outfit her sister picked out for her, sourced more from Vivi's closet than her own.

"I told you it would fit," Vivi had said with great satisfaction when she'd finished her handiwork back at the flat. "It's quite Cinderella, isn't it?"

"If Cinderella was a bit of a tart."

Eleanor ran her hands over the slinky, stretchy

dress that gave her curves absolutely nowhere to hide. For the seventeenth time, and it still accomplished nothing. She was still all breasts and hips. There was only one person alive who had ever made her feel beautiful—

But there was no use thinking about Hugo. The sooner she accepted that, the better. He wouldn't have wanted to deal with an overly sentimental virgin for long anyway. That was what Eleanor kept telling herself. No one liked clingy, especially in an employee. Vivi's tabloid story had only hastened the inevitable.

Strange how that failed to make her feel any better.

"There's nothing wrong with a tart," Vivi had admonished her, then flashed one of her grins. "It's all in the quality of the pastry, I promise you."

Eleanor didn't know what that meant. Or, rather, she opted not to pick up on her sister's innuendo. What she did know, within seconds of entering the club, was that she was most certainly too old for this scene. Perhaps not chronologically. But she had nothing in common with the blissed-out, gleaming creatures who danced madly and drank deeply and didn't seem remotely aware of the fact that there was a world outside where people were already tucked up in their beds, ready for the next morning.

And yet, as soon as she recognized that she wasn't built to enjoy flinging back spirits and then leaping around the dance floor like Geraldine on too much sugar, she really rather enjoyed herself. It was too loud to worry about Hugo. It was too dark to worry about herself and what on earth she planned to do with her life. It was too noisy and too chaotic to do more than smile and then duck away from the strange men who tried to speak to her now and again.

Maybe tottering around town on a random Wednesday was exactly the medicine she needed, come to think of it. Eleanor decided it was, and let the night wash over her.

It was coming on three in the morning when Vivi was finally ready to leave her pack of posh friends and their innumerable dramas. Eleanor was quite pleased with herself for contriving to keep her eyes open the whole of the night, even if she'd lapsed into a strange state where she couldn't tell if she was actually asleep or not. It hadn't seemed to make much of a difference.

Vivi was chattering, as much to herself as anyone else as far as Eleanor could tell, about summoning a taxi driver with her mobile and about which of her circle she'd rowed with over the course of the evening. And Eleanor let it all wash over her, too. Because yes, she thought she really was half-asleep. But also, none of this felt like life. None of it felt real.

London didn't fit her anymore. The thought slid into her head and stayed there, taking up space. Growing with every breath. She had no idea what she was going do about that, because the only place she'd felt as if she'd fit, she'd lost. Yorkshire was as closed to her as if there was a wall around it and several armies keeping her out.

Stop, she ordered herself. *Stop thinking about Hugo.*

"I cannot imagine what you think you're doing, Miss Andrews."

Eleanor froze. Surely that voice was only in her head, the way it had been all week—but no. It was still going.

"Role models for proper young ladies, the wards of dukes, no less, cannot be carousing in the streets of London at this hour. Whatever would the tabloids say?"

That voice was straight from her dreams. It couldn't be real. Eleanor didn't react—but Vivi did. She froze solid next to her.

And Eleanor let herself believe what was right before her eyes, a car or two down from where she and Vivi had exited the club.

Hugo.

CHAPTER FOURTEEN

Of course it was Hugo.

He lounged at the curb next to a gleaming sports car that was as sleek and muscular—and expensive—as he was. It was hard to tell the difference between them. Both seemed to light up the dark all around them with the same kind of danger.

She'd dreamed this a thousand times since she'd left Groves House, but now it was happening and Eleanor didn't know what to say. What could she possibly say?

"Hugo…" she whispered.

The Duke straightened, pushing away from his leaning position against the side of the powerful vehicle. He looked elegant and dangerous with the streets of London arrayed there behind him, as if his presence rendered the ancient, ever-settled city as wild and untamed as the moors up north. His dark gaze was almost too hot to bear.

And he focused on Eleanor as if she was the only other person for miles.

For a moment she thought she was.

Then Vivi cleared her throat, and Eleanor felt reality slap her again. Hard.

"I'm sure you must be very angry," Vivi began, looking and sounding as uncertain as Eleanor felt. At a later point, she might reflect on the fact that she'd never actually heard her sister sound remorseful before. But at the moment, she was too busy greedily drinking in the sight of Hugo. Right there in front of her and who cared how.

"I don't get angry," Hugo said in that low way of his that made everything inside Eleanor seemed to run liquid and hot, then shudder before starting all over again. "What is another scandalous story in the tabloids to me? One fiction after the next, without end. One life destroyed by my touch only to appear in a bathing costume in Ibiza the following summer on the arm of a film star. Who can keep track?"

It was the cynicism in his voice that almost killed her, Eleanor thought. The weariness. It felt like a knife straight into her gut.

Because she remembered. She remembered what it had been like in his bedchamber that night. She remembered the look on his beautiful face then. Open. Filled with longing and wonder and almost too much light to bear.

"You should keep track," Eleanor heard herself say, just as she heard the huskiness in her voice that she was sure told him far too much. Gave too much away. Made her far too vulnerable. She didn't care. "Someone should keep track. Someday you will make a note of all the lies and I wouldn't be surprised if apologies followed."

Beside her, she felt Vivi tense, but she couldn't spare a glance for her sister. Not now.

"Don't be so naïve," Hugo murmured, all weary cynicism and a bit of censure besides, as if he was in some snide ballroom making cutting remarks behind a quizzing glass, like the Dukes in Eleanor's favorite novels. And yet his voice seemed to fill the street, then reverberate around inside of her, too. "There are never any apologies. *Especially* when the lies are proven to be falsehoods. No one cares about that. They care about the story, and the more salacious and slanderous it is, the better."

Eleanor stepped in front of Vivi then, because the tension in the air felt like a weapon. "It's not her fault. She was taking care of me."

Hugo smirked, and it made Eleanor flinch.

"Because I am the big bad wolf, after all," he agreed in that same dark way. "Despoiler of maidens when they are so unfortunate as to cross my path. Hunkered down in my Yorkshire cave, picking my teeth with the bones of my enemies."

"It is because you say things like that with such obvious relish," Eleanor pointed out crisply, "that it's difficult to imagine you are anything else."

"I'm not sorry," Vivi said over Eleanor's shoulder. Unwisely, in Eleanor's opinion. "Everyone knows what you're like. If you've come down here to bully us, or make things difficult because of the story, you should know that I'm more than capable of taking care of Eleanor as well as myself."

"Are you now?" Hugo's smirk could have taken chunks out of the old, listed building behind them. Eleanor was surprised it still stood. Or that she did. "Let me guess. You will smile prettily. Eleanor will frown. And before you will fall the whole of London and assorted villains just like me. With a click of your fingers."

Hugo didn't wait for an answer to that. He did that thing with his hand again. He merely lifted it, and just like that a cab came screeching to a halt in front of him. He moved from front of his own sports car to the cab, and opened the passenger door with great flourish.

"Your carriage awaits," he said.

Eleanor blinked. It seemed absurd to her that Hugo would appear before her at three o'clock in the morning only to summon them a taxi, but maybe Vivi was more right than she'd wanted to accept. Maybe men were in fact this mystifying at all times. She set her teeth in that way that was becoming a little too common, straightened her shoulders to match, and she marched toward the cab.

"Not you," Hugo said, a current of something like laughter in his voice. Or maybe Eleanor was so desperate to pretend he didn't hate her that she was imagining it. Either way, he reached out a hand and hooked her arm. "You're coming with me."

Vivi stopped on Eleanor's other side. "Oh, no,

she's not. Don't go after the weak link. If you want a fight, fight me."

And Eleanor stood there on a London street in the middle of a Wednesday night that had long since become a Thursday morning, her sister fierce at her back and this maddening, intoxicating, gorgeous man before her.

It seemed as if her whole life had come down to this moment. Did she fall back into what was comfortable and let Vivi do her thing the way she always did—the way she'd done when she'd left Yorkshire without a word to Hugo, in fact? Or did she step forward into all the blistering unknown she could see shining there in Hugo's eyes—whether he hated her as he should…or didn't?

How would she live with herself if she didn't try?

There was a part of her that wanted to wait and see. She wanted to see who Hugo would choose. This wasn't a ballroom, in the middle of the night, empty of everyone save the two of them. This was a London street, and both she and Vivi were dressed for the night they'd just had. That meant skin. Skin and lean, lanky attractiveness on Vivi's part. Skin and abundant curves on Eleanor's.

There was a part of her that wanted to act as if she and her sister were a buffet. Line them both up and watch him as he made his decision, so she could see if she was the one he'd chose because she was convenient, or because he really was the only man she'd ever met who wanted her, not her sister.

And she was tired of everyone around her making

decisions for her. Even if they were well-meaning. Even if the decisions were in her best interest.

Maybe it was time for Eleanor to make a choice herself.

"It's okay," she said. She kept her eyes trained on Hugo, but she squeezed her sister's hand. "You can go Vivi. Really."

"But—"

"Go," she said again, with soft certainty. "I'll see you at home."

There must have been something in her tone, then, that brooked no disobedience. Or any back talk. Vivi squeezed her hand back, hard, and then got into the waiting car. She slammed the door behind her, and the cab headed off, chugging down the street and then around the corner.

And Eleanor was left standing on a quiet street in a busy city, with the man she never thought she'd see again. Not face to face. Not anywhere but in her head and on a screen or a glossy tabloid page.

"Eleanor. Little one." Hugo shook his head, and it made heat spiral through her, charging through her where she stood as if he'd lit a match. Making the heels she wore seem that much more precarious. "Whatever are you wearing?"

"In comparison to most of the girls I saw tonight, I might as well be wearing a grandmother's cardi and a suit of armor."

"A suit of armor would be a good start."

"I'm wearing a perfectly lovely dress, thank you," Eleanor said primly, and kept herself from tugging on the hem of it by sheer force of will. "If I was working, I'd be wearing something appropriate for work."

"Your hair."

His voice sounded almost tortured, and Eleanor stopped breathing. He reached out and raked his fingers through the dark mass that Vivi had made wavy and thick.

"I hate your hair up, Eleanor. Have I told you that?"

"It's a good job it isn't up to you, then. Isn't it?"

"Are you certain it isn't up to me?"

Hugo moved closer, but all Eleanor could feel was what hung there between them. That tabloid story. Eleanor's innocence. Geraldine. Or the fact she was in love with him, just like a silly, clingy virgin in a story who didn't know enough to guard her own heart. Too many things to bear.

But Hugo moved closer as if he was as entranced she was. As if he couldn't stay away. And Eleanor stopped thinking about anything but him and the half smile on his face as he looked down at her.

"Maybe you haven't heard. I'm a great and glorious peer of the realm. My every wish is law. Or close enough."

He shifted closer. He moved so he could cup her face in his hands, his hundred-percent-proof eyes intent on hers. And everything inside her shivered. Rocked a little bit, then rolled, deep and low.

And this time, she didn't think it was the shoes.

"The tabloids…" She whispered. "Hugo, I'm so

very sorry. I don't know how I can ever make it right."

"I don't care about the tabloids."

Eleanor scowled at him. "Well, you should. It's not a small thing to have all these lies told about you. You should care and you should fight and you should—"

"But that's the thing. In this case, the tabloids are no more than the truth. I did take advantage of you. You worked for me and I shouldn't have touched you. But I did."

"I wanted you to."

"I didn't say I was sorry."

He shifted again, and there was a look on his face that Eleanor thought she'd seen before, though she couldn't quite place it. And then it came to her. It had been that night. Locked away in his bedchamber, just the two of them, with nothing outside his door between them. He'd propped himself over her, he'd sunk himself deep inside of her, and he'd looked at her. Just like this.

Her heart began to beat at her, slow and intense.

"I forgot how to fight," Hugo said. "At first I didn't care. And then I did care, but I thought I was taking the high road. And then the high road somehow became this endless act of self-immolation, acted out in the public eye as if that might make it better. It never occurred to me that the flames would take over. Or that my own father would burn."

"It wasn't your fault," she said fiercely. "This was

something that was done *to* you. You shouldn't beat yourself up for the things you did to survive it."

"I'm a selfish man, little one. I want to believe you because it's convenient, not because I think it's true."

"You are not a monster." Eleanor poked her finger in his chest as punctuation, and saw that hint of a smile deepen. It was like the sun coming out. "If anyone's a monster, it's that Isobel."

"I think you're letting me off the hook," Hugo said, his voice serious again. Too serious. "And I like that about you. But the truth is, I was callous. Unfeeling. There were any number of ways I could have handled Isobel at the start to avoid all of this, but I didn't. I suspect I must have hurt her, deeply."

"That's no excuse."

"It's an explanation."

Hugo blew out a breath. Eleanor started to say something else, but he laughed then.

"You need to stop defending me, Eleanor. I'm trying to tell you what I should have realized sooner. I love you."

All the air went out of Eleanor's body. She was too hot. Too cold.

She thought it was a fever.

Or possibly joy.

"Yes," Hugo said, as if he knew every last inch of her insecure little soul. "You." There was a wondering look on his face, and she thought his hands weren't entirely steady as they smoothed over her hair to settle at the nape of her neck. "I was so busy thinking of myself as a dragon in a cave, spouting off fire nonsense whenever anyone dared approach. And then you came. And you didn't see a dragon. You didn't see a duke. You saw a man. An irritating man, if memory serves."

"Surely not, Your Grace." But her voice was barely a whisper. Barely a scratch of sound against the night.

"You treated me like a person, nothing more. Even though you read all the same tabloid stories as anyone else. You took my ward under your wing, and more than that, stood up for her. You actually put her first."

"That's the job."

"You would be shocked how few of Geraldine's governesses considered her at all. You made a lost child feel found, Eleanor." His dark eyes gleamed. "And you made a lost man feel whole. For a few short weeks, and one long night, I completely forgot that I'm meant to be the boogeyman."

Eleanor shook her head at that, her eyes feeling much too full. "I had no idea Vivi was going to do that, Hugo. You have to believe me."

"I never fought before," he told her, his voice low and intense. "I never stood up for myself. But I'll be damned if those rags will drag you through the dirt. I've already had my attorneys contact them. I am the Duke of Grovesmoor. And I am finished hiding."

"Hugo…"

"And more importantly, I love you." He laughed, and it was a sound so pure, so filled with life and light, that Eleanor forgot it was the middle of the night. "I didn't care enough to fight before, because

I never loved Isobel. She was an annoyance, but she never hurt me. I only recognized how much I loved my own father after he died, disappointed in me to the end. I worked so hard to pretend I didn't care about my best friend or the fact he chose Isobel over me. And I decided I'd be damned if I'd soften toward the little girl he and Isobel left in my care. The truth of it was, I was fine."

Eleanor didn't realize that tears had started to slide down her face until Hugo wiped them away. She felt caught in a tight, hot grip. Unable to speak. Unable to do anything but float there, gleaming bright and buoyant.

And Hugo was still talking.

"But then you appeared. You marched up my drive in that ridiculous coat and you ruined everything. In the best possible way."

Eleanor ran her hands up the wall of his chest, indulging herself.

"What's the matter with my coat?" She tipped her head back and frowned at him. "It's very warm, Hugo."

That made him laugh again, and then he was picking her up and spinning her around and around, as if she was weightless. But then, he made her feel that way when her feet were on the ground.

"I don't know how to be anything but everyone's favorite monster," he told her when he stopped spinning them, though he still held her there against him in the cool, close night. "But I want to try. I want to watch you frown at me for the rest of my life. I want your dry tone and your prim little remarks and Eleanor, you need to understand me on this, I want everything."

"I loved you the moment I saw you," she told him, smiling down at him as her tears fell freely, and not a single one of them because she was sad. "On that terrible horse."

"Everything," he said again, as if he thought she might have missed it. "A ring on your finger and my babies in your belly, to start. After that, who knows? We can take over the world. I have no doubt you could topple a regime or two in a few weeks, if you put your mind to it. You did it to me."

"I don't want to do anything unless Geraldine's okay with it," Eleanor said, biting her lip as she considered his ward. "The poor thing doesn't need to feel any more abandoned."

"Geraldine will never be abandoned again." Hugo's words rang out like a vow. "She and I have come to an understanding, you see." He leaned forward and pressed his mouth to hers. "We can't rustle around in that great big house without you, Eleanor. It doesn't work. We need you. *I* need you."

"Your Grace," Eleanor whispered, wrapping her arms around this man who could never be a monster, not to her. "You know your wish has always been my command."

He kissed her on that lonely street, with only the faraway stars as witness, and tossed them straight on into forever.

And then, together, they found their way home.

* * *

Hugo married his governess in the spring, when Groves House was bursting with flowers and life, and even the screeching tabloids were as nothing next to the benevolent sunlight of a pretty Yorkshire afternoon.

Geraldine stood in as Hugo's Best Man, which was appropriate on a number of levels. Vivi was Eleanor's Maid of Honor, and it was interesting how she'd changed, Hugo thought. The new Vivi didn't have to worry about making connections or finding a husband or whatever plan it was the sisters had cooked up all those years ago.

"That's a terrible plan," Hugo had said when they'd laid it all out for him after Christmas that first year, probably because everyone was a touch too merry after their sumptuous dinner. "The worst I've ever heard."

The adults had been sitting about like overstuffed lords and ladies of old in one of Hugo's salons, waiting for their meals to digest a bit so they could stuff in a few more mince pies. Geraldine had been lying in front of the fire, her face in a book.

It was, Hugo had reflected with some surprise, the happiest Christmas he could recall. Ever.

"It's a plan that's worked to change the circumstances of impoverished women since the dawn of time," Eleanor had pointed out.

"It has significant downsides," Hugo had argued. "First and foremost, the rich man in question always knows exactly why he was found so marriageable. Believe me, he'll demand payment for that. Forever."

"There is always some form of payment," Vivi had said quietly. "That's just life."

Eleanor and Hugo had exchanged a look, but neither one of them had said anything—out loud—about that weary cynicism in Vivi's voice.

Later, when they were alone in the rooms that Hugo had moved her into shortly after he'd taken her home from London and put the Grovesmoor emerald on her finger, Eleanor had settled herself astride him and smiled down into his face.

"Is this part of my payment plan?" she'd asked mischievously.

"Of course." Hugo had run his hands along the crease where her thigh met her hip. "I'll insist on certain sexual favors, to be spelled out in the marriage contract."

"I have only one condition," Eleanor had said, very solemnly, angling herself down so her breasts filled his greedy palms and both of them could feel how slick and ready she was for him, as always.

"Name it."

"Love me," she demanded. "Forever."

On his wedding day, Hugo found that promising her exactly that came easily. So easily he laughed at the tabloids that called him all manner of names. So easily that he found even Vivi amusing, as she seemed to veer between finding the fact her sister had become Hugo's duchess romantic and armoring herself in that world-weariness she seemed infinitely more comfortable with.

"She'll come around," Eleanor said confidently on the dance floor as they'd moved together where everyone could watch them, in that ballroom where everything had changed between them previous autumn. Tonight she was dressed in a white gown and she wore his ring, but he could still see her the way she'd been then, with her hair down and her feet bare. "How can she help herself?"

Time changed everything, Hugo discovered. First Vivi, who took a solid year to relax around him. Then another year to really become comfortable in her new role, as a woman of some means with a very powerful brother-in-law.

"It's amazing how many people I thought I wanted to talk to when I was poor," Hugo overheard her telling Eleanor one lazy weekend in France at Hugo's vineyard. "And how little it turns out I like them now that they're the ones pursuing me."

"Imagine," Eleanor replied with a laugh. "You can spend time with only the people you like now."

And so, Hugo realized, could he.

He stopped paying attention to the papers, the way he should have years ago. He cultivated what friendships he had left, gratified to discover that those who'd truly known him had never believed the stories about him. And he let his beautiful wife guide him, with her quiet resolve and her cheerful determination, away from bitterness. More and more with each day that passed.

She knew the names of every staff member in his employ within a month. She continued Geraldine's schooling herself because she liked it. She quickly became popular in the village, with the no-nonsense demeanor good Yorkshire folk appreciated and that kindness of hers that Hugo thought could set the world alight. She took over some of the managerial aspects of the estate, because her keen mind and attention to detail far outstripped that of some of Hugo's aides.

She even built a bridge with the dour Mrs. Redding.

"She allowed as how she didn't trust me *before*," Eleanor told him, laughing, wrapped around him in their bed as she reported the conversation, "because the women ran all over you like water and none with a single thought about anything but themselves."

"Exactly the image I wish to have implanted in my wife's head."

"And then, of course, she waited to see if I drained the family coffers and attempted to divorce you for half of what wasn't mine."

"As well you should. There was no prenup. You have the Grovesmoor fortune entirely within your control, little one."

Eleanor pressed her mouth against his chest, sending a new heat spiraling through him. And that deeper weight that had nothing to do with sex, but everything to do with her. His miraculous Eleanor. "It's not the fortune I want to control. Just the Duke."

"He's a lost cause."

But he was laughing as he said it, and he grinned at Eleanor when she frowned at him.

"No," she said crisply, "he is not. And more, he never was."

And the more time passed, the more he believed it. Isobel had only ever told stories. Torquil might have believed them, but both of them had paid far too high a price for that.

Hugo didn't need to pay it, too. Not anymore.

And he certainly didn't intend to let Geraldine pay a single penny.

She was nine when she got her hands on the tabloids they'd deliberately kept from her for years.

"Is it true?" she asked, her fierce little face screwed up tight, as if she was keeping herself from sobbing by will alone. "Do you keep me only to get revenge on my mother?"

"How would that work, exactly?" Hugo asked mildly. He and Eleanor were reading in his library, but he noticed Eleanor kept very still. Letting the little girl speak to him directly. "I suppose I could lock you in a cupboard, if that would help. Beneath a stair, perhaps?"

"Do you hate me?" Geraldine had asked. She'd looked at him full on , and there was no mistaking the fact that she was a nine-year-old then, no matter how precocious she seemed at other times.

And this was how Hugo knew that Eleanor had changed him, from the inside out. He remembered sitting in opposite chairs from his ward and deciding that they should get Eleanor back. But that Hugo had been handicapped by his own distrust of everything. This Hugo knew what love was. He lived it every day.

So he reached out and pulled the little girl onto his lap, where she belonged.

"You are my ward by law," he told her gruffly, liking the weight of her solid little body against his. Liking the feeling that rose in him, thick and real, that told him he would protect this child against the world with his own hands if necessary. "But as far as I'm concerned, Geraldine, you have always been my daughter."

And as she snuggled into him he lifted his head, and saw Eleanor wiping tears away across from him, her face wreathed in smiles.

A year or so after that, Geraldine pushed her way into the library one summer evening, already slouching about as she walked, like the teenager she would be entirely too soon for Hugo's peace of mind.

"I'm certain I've asked you to knock," Hugo said mildly, his attention on the drink in his hand and his lovely wife, who was frowning intently over the book in her lap. Eleanor had decided to get the university degree she'd been too busy to get when she'd been younger, and was spending the summer with a reading list.

Hugo wasn't sure it was physically possible to love her more.

Geraldine held his gaze. "Knock, knock," she said, because she was as smart-mouthed as anyone else in this house.

"Charming," Hugo murmured.

"I've thought about it and I've come to a decision," Geraldine told him.

"Have you changed your mind about school?" Eleanor asked, lifting her head.

"I still want to go," Geraldine replied. "It will be fun to board and I'll come home all the time. But you two will be so lonely without me."

Hugo's mouth twitched. "Indeed."

Eleanor's dark eyes danced, but she nodded seriously. "I'm sure that's true."

"Well, I know what you need to do," Geraldine said, and then she smiled. "You need to have a baby. As soon as possible."

And Hugo would never know how both he and Eleanor kept from laughing at that, but they didn't. They thanked Geraldine and then, when she'd skipped back out again to enjoy the long, blue evening, they'd dissolved into the laughter they'd been holding at bay.

But they obeyed her.

Ten months later, the Duke was delighted to catch his first son and heir as he roared his way into the world. But not, perhaps, as delighted as his ward, who was sure she'd plotted out the whole thing.

And Eleanor had never done one thing when she could do three instead. That was how the future Duke of Grovesmoor found himself with a little brother and a baby sister in short order, all of them loud and rowdy and perfect.

"Look at that," Eleanor said as she shepherded

their little brood through the village on a blustery sort of fall afternoon that reminded Hugo of the day they'd met. She was even wearing that hideous puffy coat of hers, that she'd steadfastly refused to throw away no matter how many glorious, sleek, and flattering coats he'd gifted her with over the years. Obstinate woman. "I hardly recognize the man in those headlines."

Hugo glanced over at the newsstand and saw his own face, but didn't bother to read whatever nonsense they'd spouted about him this time. He took his wife's hand in his and raised it to his mouth. His sons were running ahead of him toward the green, chasing Geraldine who was for all intents and purposes their older sister, and he was holding his baby girl against his chest.

"Ah, little one," he said with a deep and quiet contentment that was pressed down into his bones now, a part of him forever. "I don't believe in ghosts."

His family was complete. His heart was whole.

Eleanor looked at him as if he'd always been the man she was so proud of, and Hugo believed, at last, that he was.

And would be for as long as they were together—which would be for the rest of their natural lives and far beyond if he had anything to say about it.

Which he bloody well did. He was the Duke of Grovesmoor, after all.

* * * * *

If you enjoyed
UNDONE BY THE BILLIONAIRE DUKE
why not explore these other stories
by Caitlin Crews?

THE GUARDIAN'S VIRGIN WARD
BRIDE BY ROYAL DECREE
THE PRINCE'S NINE-MONTH SCANDAL
THE BILLIONAIRE'S SECRET PRINCESS

Available now!

#3573 THE GREEK'S FORBIDDEN PRINCESS
The Princess Seductions
by Annie West

Tragedy brings the press swarming around Princess Amelie, so she takes her nephew and runs to Lambis Evangelos for protection. His desire for Amelie is incredible, but he's always refused to taint her. Until Amelie's forbidden temptation arrives at his doorstep...

#3574 VALDEZ'S BARTERED BRIDE
Convenient Christmas Brides
by Rachael Thomas

The only way for Lydia to absolve her father's horrifying debts is to accept Raul Valdez's outrageous proposition. She must help him claim his inheritance—or marry Raul on Christmas Eve! Lydia finds she cannot resist her desire for the dark-hearted billionaire...!

#3575 KIDNAPPED FOR THE TYCOON'S BABY
Secret Heirs of Billionaires
by Louise Fuller

Nola Mason doesn't expect to see Ramsay Walker again after their explosive fling, never considering the consequences! Ram must claim his heir—he'll steal her away to his rain-forest hideaway and use their heat-fuelled passion to entice her into marriage!

#3576 A NIGHT, A CONSEQUENCE, A VOW
Ruthless Billionaire Brothers
by Angela Bissell

Emily Royce needs Ramon de la Vega's investment to save her business. But Ramon's piercing gaze reveals their potent chemistry—and one glorious night in Paris results in pregnancy! Ramon will make her his any way he can. Even with his ring!

YOU CAN FIND MORE INFORMATION ON UPCOMING HARLEQUIN® TITLES, FREE EXCERPTS AND MORE AT WWW.HARLEQUIN.COM.

HPCNM1017RB

SPECIAL EXCERPT FROM

HARLEQUIN
Presents

*When chauffeur Keira Ryan drives into a snowdrift, she and
her devastatingly attractive passenger must find a hotel…
but there's only one bed! Luckily, Matteo Valenti knows how
to make the best of a bad situation—with the most sizzling
experience of her life. It's nearly Christmas again before
Matteo uncovers Keira's secret. He's avoided commitment
his whole life, but now it's time to claim his heir…*

Read on for a sneak preview of
Sharon Kendrick's book
THE ITALIAN'S CHRISTMAS SECRET

One Night With Consequences

"Santino?" Matteo repeated, wondering if he'd misheard her.
He stared at her, his brow creased in a frown. "You gave him
an Italian name?"

"Yes."

"Why?"

"Because when I looked at him—" Keira's voice faltered as
she scraped her fingers back through her hair and turned those
big sapphire eyes on him "—I knew I could call him nothing
else but an Italian name."

"Even though you sought to deny him his heritage and kept
his birth hidden from me?"

She swallowed. "You made it very clear that you never
wanted to see me again, Matteo."

His voice grew hard. "I haven't come here to argue the
rights and wrongs of your secrecy. I've come to see my son."

It was a demand Keira couldn't ignore. She'd seen the brief
tightening of his face when she'd mentioned his child and
another wave of guilt had washed over her.

HPEXP1017

"Come with me," she said huskily.

He followed her up the narrow staircase and Keira was acutely aware of his presence behind her. She could detect the heat from his body and the subtle sandalwood that was all his and, stupidly, she remembered the way that scent had clung to her skin the morning after he'd made love to her. Her heart was thundering by the time they reached the room she shared with Santino and she held her breath as Matteo stood frozen for a moment before moving soundlessly toward the crib.

"Matteo?" she said.

Matteo didn't answer. Not then. He wasn't sure he trusted himself to speak because his thoughts were in such disarray. He stared down at the dark fringe of eyelashes that curved on the infant's olive-hued cheeks and the shock of black hair. Tiny hands were curled into two tiny fists and he found himself leaning forward to count all the fingers, nodding his head with satisfaction as he registered each one.

He swallowed.

His *son*.

He opened his mouth to speak but Santino chose that moment to start to whimper and Keira bent over the crib to scoop him up. "Would you...would you like to hold him?"

"Not now," he said abruptly. "There isn't time. You need to pack your things while I call ahead and prepare for your arrival in Italy."

"What?"

"You heard me. You can't put out a call for help and then ignore help when it comes. You telephoned me and now you must accept the consequences," he added grimly.

Don't miss
THE ITALIAN'S CHRISTMAS SECRET
available November 2017 wherever
Harlequin Presents® books and ebooks are sold.

www.Harlequin.com

Want to give in to temptation with
steamy tales of irresistible desire?

Check out **Harlequin® Presents®**,
Harlequin® Desire and
Harlequin® Kimani™ Romance books!

New books available every month!

CONNECT WITH US AT:

Harlequin.com/Community

 Facebook.com/HarlequinBooks

Twitter.com/HarlequinBooks

Instagram.com/HarlequinBooks

Pinterest.com/HarlequinBooks

ReaderService.com

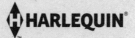 **HARLEQUIN®**

**ROMANCE WHEN
YOU NEED IT**

PGENRE2017

⟨H⟩ HARLEQUIN

Presents®

Next month, Harlequin Presents welcomes you to the passionate world of Abby Green's new duet—Rulers of the Desert! Powerful monarchs Zafir and Salim have never had their wishes challenged—until they meet the women they're determined to take to their beds. Kat and Charlotte might find their seduction to be irresistible... But to claim them truly, their seducers must make them their desert queens!

Sheikh Zafir Al-Noury cannot forgive model Kat Winters for breaking off their engagement—but neither can he forget their burning-hot nights together. Hiring her to promote his kingdom's most famous jewel creates an opportunity for renewed seduction...

Walking away from Zafir devastated Kat. The pain has made her strong, but the fire he ignites is stronger yet—Zafir tempts her to complete sensual surrender! Even if that means exposing every part of herself to the man who once ruled her soul...

A Diamond for the Sheikh's Mistress

Available now

A Christmas Bride for the King

Coming soon

HPBPA1017